ZULU

Steel Patriots MC

Book Four

Mary Kennedy

III
INSATIABLE INK

CHAPTER ONE

Quincy "Zulu" Slater stood before the military action and disciplinary review board, his hands held stiffly at his sides. The gold trident on his chest gleamed in the early morning sunlight filtering into the room, the ribbons on his breast lined up neatly, precisely as regulations demanded. It was over one hundred degrees, but he willed himself not to sweat in front of the men seated before him.

There should be no reason his team should all be here, pleading a case before this review board that the review board itself sent the team out on and determined what the outcome should be. None of them should be standing in this room defending themselves for a mission completed. Twelve innocent little schoolgirls stolen from their school, tortured, raped, beaten, and left hanging on the side of the cliff. Zulu and his teammates were sent to free the girls, bring them home, and kill the terrorists.

They found the girls hanging from that cliff, their tiny, bloated bodies being desecrated by buzzards and vultures. They cut them down, wrapped their little bodies, and sent them home to their parents. Then they went in search of the terrorists.

Zulu remembered every single moment of the three-day trek. He'd gotten his call sign, Zulu, because Zulu was the last letter of the call alphabet, and he, as the biggest member of their team, always brought up the rear, taking out any stray bad guys as he went. Some would say he also received the call sign because, as the biggest man on the team, he was always the last in line for pictures, food, and anything requiring height/weight proportion alignment. It didn't matter to him. Zulu was way better than Quincy in his mind.

The team found the men responsible for the girls' deaths inside a small hut near a river. One guard was on the outside, barely even awake. He'd like to say he handled him appropriately, whatever the fuck that meant, but he didn't. He gripped his throat with one of his massive hands and squeezed the life out of him—literally.

At six-foot-six and two hundred and eighty pounds of pure muscle, Zulu was bigger than most of his teammates, but it was his natural, pure strength that set him apart in a fight. As with any SEAL, he was adept with a wide variety of weapons, but for Zulu, his hands were preferred when applicable.

Zulu's team lead, Eric "Ghost" Stanton, was also a Navy Seal, but the team was made up of various members of the Special Forces community. They were a team of elite warriors hand-selected by Ghost and the government to take on missions that regular teams couldn't or wouldn't take on.

Loyalty to country, team, and teammate

Serve with honor and integrity on and off the battlefield

Ready to lead, ready to follow, never quit

Take responsibility for your actions and the actions of your teammates

Excel as warriors through discipline and innovation

Train for war, fight to win, defeat our nation's enemies

Earn your trident every day.

Zulu recited the SEAL code in his head, after each statement asking himself if he had held up the code on this mission, and at the end of each of those statements, he replied with a loud 'hell yea' in his head.

"Chief Petty Officer Slater?"

"Sorry, sir," he said, staring at the man, "could you please repeat the question?"

"I asked if you believed there were any other options, other than the course of action you and the team took in this instance?" said Admiral Crossing.

"No, sir, I do not," said Zulu. "We were faced with an unconscionable act of violence. The intel we received was incorrect. Those terrorists did not want a ransom. They wanted those children for their own perverse uses. Had we known that sooner, we would have moved more quickly and taken action faster. However, we were not given that information."

Zulu stared directly at the Army intelligence officer who had been responsible for feeding the team the information on the mission. He knew it wasn't ransom these assholes were after. Those poor girls came from families with barely enough money to buy their school uniforms. If they had known, the speed at which they conducted the mission would have been very different.

"Is it your belief then, Chief Petty Officer, that you and your team did not go rogue on this mission?" asked General Whitman.

"Rogue, sir?" questioned Zulu with a hard stare. "We did exactly as we were told, sir – exactly. We recovered those children, sent them home to be buried by their mothers' and fathers', and we found the enemy. We did not go rogue, sir."

"It's a matter of opinion," murmured the Air Force colonel.

"Opinion, sir?" said Zulu. Crossing started to speak, but Zulu proceeded with his tirade. "Sir, I don't pretend to have an opinion about what you had for breakfast this morning because I wasn't there. I don't pretend to have an opinion about whether you should have chosen the Air Force over the Marines because I wasn't there. I don't pretend to have an opinion that you married the right woman or wrong woman. Because. I. Wasn't. There. I would respectfully state, sir, you were not there."

"If you can look me in the eye, if you can all look me in the eye and say that seeing a dozen tiny, innocent little girls swinging from a cliff wouldn't affect you, well then forgive me for my insolence." Zulu was ready to explode, and Crossing knew it. He was a good man, and the team was somewhat relieved when they saw his face on the panel. But the assholes sitting beside him were a waste of space, in Zulu's opinion.

"Chief Petty Officer, do you regret your actions?"

"I regret nothing, sir, absolutely nothing. I hope that not another child will be taken and treated the way those girls were because of our actions. Because you can be damned sure the next terrorist will think twice before doing anything like that knowing that me and my teammates are out there."

"Thank you, CPO Slater," said Crossing. "You can step outside and wait with your teammates while we finish with the others."

Zulu stepped into the hallway and took his seat next to Whiskey, not saying a word. Whiskey gave a small smirk his way and then was called next to testify, and then Jack "Doc" Harris was called after him as they waited calmly for him to return.

Because of the shitty construction of the building, they could hear everything being said inside the room, and when Jack "Doc" Harris notified the members of the panel that he possessed photos of the girls, they all stirred a bit in their seats. Taking photos of prisoners, dead bodies, anything to do with a mission was strictly forbidden unless directed to do so. Doc could be placing a noose on all their necks, or he could be saving them.

Doc stepped outside the room and stared at his teammates, nodding at them to walk with him to the end of the hallway.

"Fucking hell, Doc, we didn't know you had photos," said Ghost.

"I know. I took them when we were cutting the girls down. Don't ask me why. I know it's a violation, but I just had this feeling, and shit for luck, it paid off."

"Well," said Razor, "I, for one, am fucking eternally grateful. They won't court-martial us with the fear of those photos becoming public. The liberals would be screaming about human rights, and the conservatives would say the killing of those men was justified. They don't want to have to argue that."

"This shit is getting fucking exhausting," said Ghost. "I'm so damned tired of having to follow rules created by men who don't do the damn job anymore, or, for that matter, ever did the job." They all nodded as the doors of the hearing room opened once again. The MP waved them inside.

Standing before the committee, the men all removed their hats and stood at attention.

"Gentlemen, you have presented us with a dilemma, and I won't lie. It's one I hate," said Admiral Crossing. "Your work as a unit has been indisputable, but we are getting pressures from the country's government claiming you murdered innocent men."

Zulu looked at the Admiral, almost asking for permission to speak but thought better of it.

"I didn't say I agree. However, we are tasked with making a show of, hell, I don't even know anymore. We are asking you to retire, gentlemen. If you refuse, you will be dishonorably discharged. If you take the retirement, there will be no mark on your records. It saddens me to do this, to lose some of the finest men I know, and that I know we need in our service."

It seemed like a no-brainer, but Whiskey was pissed that he was being forced out because of their fear of some shithole government.

"I accept retirement," said Zulu through clenched jaw.

The chorus was heard down the line as each man agreed, regrettably. The Admiral nodded at them, handing them their papers that would tell administration they were taking retirement, effective immediately.

"You will be expected to be packed and on the next transport home within forty-eight hours. I wish you good luck, men. The world needs people like you. I hope you find a way to continue to the good fight."

Zulu wanted to turn around and lay into them but knew this was not the time. He silently followed the rest of his team outside to their barracks, took his uniform off for the last time, and packed his belongings. Thirty-six hours later, they were seated on a transport discussing their futures.

"Where will you go, Ghost?" asked Whiskey. Ghost looked at the men he'd called teammates for the last decade. Each man was hand-selected for his team, partly because he knew of their skills, but mostly because he trusted them with his life and the lives of every member of the team.

"I have a proposition for all of you. I know some of you have family back home, but nobody has an old lady that I'm aware of," he said, smirking at the men on the transport.

"Well, Tango has a mule he's fond of," said Doc with a smile.

"Fuck you, Doc, at least it's a female mule," he grinned. "So, what's your point, Ghost?"

"My point is when my pops died, he left me a huge piece of land. It's nothing special, but it's got an old garage on the property where he used to repair cars, bikes, tractors, shit like that for neighbors. The house burned down years ago, but Pops made the barn into a pretty livable space."

"Sooooo, you want us all to live there?" asked Gunner.

"Like share bunk beds or some shit?" questioned Zulu.

"No, I mean, yea. Look, I ride. You all know that, and I know that most of you do too. What if... what if we formed our own club – motorcycle club? We pick a name, make the garage something that we can all work, and maybe open a bar or some shit."

The men all looked at one another, nodding. It was a good idea, but not one of them knew anything about running a business or a bar.

"I'm in," said Tango, "but I know jack-shit about operating a bar. I can fix anything with a motor, and so can most of you but a bar? I don't know, man. I know *how* to drink, just not how to mix drinks."

"Look, it doesn't have to happen right away. MCs are pretty territorial. We need to make sure we're not stepping on anyone's toes. I'm not a fan of becoming an outlaw MC. We got our taste of outlaw in that fucking shithole we just came from, and it didn't do any of us any good. I'm suggesting that between the bar and the garage, we'll have two legitimate businesses. Maybe, maybe on the side, we sort of informally help people."

"Help people? Like good Samaritans?" asked Gunner.

"Sort of, I'm thinking more like we take jobs others won't, but only the ones we want to take. We find lost kids, kidnap victims. We help the old lady being screwed over by a nasty landlord, shit like that." The men all looked at him, raising their eyebrows. "Look, I know we've spent our entire careers doing just this kind of shit, but now we get to do it on our terms. The shop needs cleaning up, and the barn will need to be made inhabitable– adding more electrical, plumbing – but it's huge. I've got a shit ton of money saved from all my deployments, and Pops left me a nice little chunk of change."

"And we'd be partners?" asked Whiskey.

"Yea, we'd be fucking partners. We'd be brothers, asshole," he said with a grin. "Just like we are now. We'd rely on one another and do shit our way. No red tape, no governments telling us what to do. We ride our fucking bikes when we want; we take the jobs we want; we fuck who we want, and we drink 'til we can't drink no more." The men smiled in his direction.

"I'm in," said Tango.

"Me too," said Doc.

"Why the fuck not?" said Razor.

"Fuck, you know I'm in, asshole," said Gunner.

"I guess we need a name," said Whiskey. "How about Steel Soldiers?"

"No fucking way, asshole. I'm a SEAL, not a fucking soldier," said Tango. The others laughed and nodded. They were all from different branches of the military and loved teasing each other about the superiority of their own branch, but deep down held mad respect for one another.

"Steel Patriots," said Ghost. "The steel between our legs and the fucking patriot spirit we all still carry."

"Steel Patriots," whispered Whiskey. The others nodded and smiled.

"Steel Patriots it is."

CHAPTER TWO

Dr. Gabrielle London checked the incision of her patient, a sixty-three-year-old woman, gently pressing her abdomen, watching for her pain level. She'd had her gallbladder removed in the middle of the night after coming in experiencing extreme abdominal pain, having ignored it for almost three days, and by the time Gabi got her into the operating room, the patient was almost septic.

"It looks good, Mrs. Martinez," she said, smiling at the woman. "If everything looks good with the labs this afternoon, you can go home. You're going to need to take it slow, move carefully. No lifting for six weeks, and a visit with the nutritionist to talk about your diet."

"Gracias, doctor," she said quietly. Gabi nodded and walked back into the hallway, headed toward the doctors' lounge after an exceptionally long shift. Sitting on the bench in front of her locker, she loaded up her bag with her street clothes, not bothering to change out of her scrubs, and stretched her back, hearing the popping and cracking of vertebrae; she headed back into the hallway, stopping at the nurses' station.

"Have a good evening, Tammy," she said, waving to the nurse. The woman was on the phone but waved back at the doctor as she disappeared out the doors. Tammy was one of the very few people who'd shown any sort of kindness to Gabi when she started at the hospital.

Gabi made her way to her older model sedan, the rusted side panels having seen much better days. Exiting the hospital parking lot, she left the main street, taking the freeway toward her small apartment outside Atlanta. It wasn't much, but it was all she needed for the time being. Ten years out of medical school, and she was finally paying off her loans and almost debt-free. A few more months in the tiny, rented apartment, and she could do whatever she wanted to do. Maybe buy a little house somewhere or treat herself to a new car.

Raised in Baltimore by two working-class parents, Gabi had been different since birth. She was extremely curious and intelligent. That wasn't so different for a child. It was her appearance. An appearance that earned her stares, gasps, and even outright gawking at the most inopportune times.

Both of her parents had dark brown hair and blue eyes, but when Gabi was born, the doctors wondered if she was some sort of freakish twist of nature or a rare form or version of an albino.

Her silvery white-blonde hair was not only thicker than usual on an infant, but also the color was striking, but it was the translucent gray eyes that unnerved everyone. At first glance, they almost glowed in the dark, but up close, they literally looked like a stormy ocean moving across the horizon. It appeared that the color was almost floating in the eye.

She didn't think twice about it anymore, well, not really, but she told herself that so as not to feel so lonely. More than a few dates were freaked by it and left their date early, or men simply didn't ask her out at all. In school, she was either seen as the rarity everyone wanted to be friends with or the freak no one wanted to touch. It really depended on what grade she was in at the time.

Initially, doctors thought she would experience vision problems, but her vision had always been twenty/twenty with no problems seeing light, color, distance, or up close. Many doctors wanted to run 'tests' on her eyes and hair, but her parents strongly refused, protecting their daughter as best they could.

She'd had a good childhood, a good life, all things considered. Her parents protected her, perhaps even over-protecting her to some degree, but their love was evident, and their concern for their daughter always forefront in their mind. But it was relationships that were the challenge.

She'd had only two serious relationships in her life, and both ended when her partner cheated. The first one, a brilliant doctor at Walter Reed, the hospital she'd done her residency, lied to her about his marital status. What he really wanted to do was experiment on those eyes and find out how they'd become so 'deformed,' along with his *wife,* another doctor, of course. That was the word he used to describe them, deformed, and of course, he forgot to mention the whole wife thing.

Yea, dumped his ass.

The second one was nothing to write home about anyway. He'd been comfortable, and they enjoyed one another's company. Of course, he enjoyed everyone else's company also. Yep. Done with that jackass as well.

Pulling into her apartment complex, she made her way upstairs, tossed her bag on the floor, and headed toward the refrigerator.

Grabbing the container of Chinese from the night before, she popped it into the microwave, set the timer, and then walked toward her bedroom.

In less than three minutes, she'd stripped, jumped in the shower to rinse off, and pulled her sweats on to eat the leftovers and get off her aching feet. Fifteen hours of standing in the emergency room were more than enough.

Gabi turned on the television but didn't really pay attention to anything being said. It was bad news, more bad news, and pending bad news. She saw enough of that in the emergency room every day.

Lately, her mind wandered to someone she shouldn't be thinking of at all. Actually, that was a lie. She'd been thinking about him for too long, not just recently. Fifteen years. It had been fifteen years since she had the most beautiful, non-sexual moment of her life. The moment she defined every encounter with afterward.

While working at Walter Reed on a surgical rotation, a hurricane came full-force straight at them. Although most of the patients had been moved to higher floors, her patient, the patient she'd successfully removed the bullet from, the bullet so close to his spine it could have paralyzed him, could not be moved. Gabi opted to stay with him the entire night, ensuring his comfort and also not wanting to leave his side.

When power was lost, she didn't panic, using the backup generator provided to her in the room for his machines. She sat next to his bed, talking to him the whole night, holding his hand, and whispering in his ear. She read him *The Hobbit* and every article in two old football magazines. Every time she looked at him, her breath caught in her chest. He was the most beautiful man she'd ever seen.

When she reached for his hand with the first loud clap of thunder, she was struck almost dumb by the contrast in their skin. Her ghostly alabaster skin next to his deep rich brown was mesmerizing. His hands were enormous, his thighs thick and rippled with muscles, but it was the rest of his body that plagued her dreams at night.

During surgery, she'd seen his abdomen, chest, back, buttocks, and yes, his dick, and she nearly gasped when she got the full view of that. It was completely unprofessional, but when the chief surgeon made a snide remark about the patient carrying a baseball bat, she knew it wasn't just her. He was huge, bigger than any man she'd ever seen.

In the midst of the worst of the winds and rain, she'd leaned over him, frightened by the thunder but pretended to adjust his pillow when he opened his eyes, staring directly at her. He lifted one of those massive hands, gripping the back of her neck with surprising strength, and pulled her to him. She couldn't have pulled away even if she wanted to. His full luscious lips pressed against hers, his tongue sliding between her teeth as his big fingers massaged her neck. When she pulled back, he looked directly at her, blinked three times, and then simply closed his eyes.

Gabi touched her lips, remembering that night so vividly. He didn't wake again while she was on shift, and that was the most disappointing part of the whole damn thing for Gabi.

Fifteen years and she still remembered his name, Quincy Slater. He was a Navy SEAL then. Maybe he still was. She thought about him for a few more minutes and realized she was making herself wet and hot.

Change of subject, Gabi. Her mind trailed back to the issue she'd discovered a few days ago, unsure of what to do or who to approach with the problem.

While randomly checking on a few patients, she'd discovered that there were inordinate numbers of patients with little to no symptoms being sent through surgery, most in the middle of the night or very early morning hours. She was never the attending surgeon, but all of them appeared to have disappeared or died. They were otherwise healthy patients. In fact, she could find no record of their final diagnosis or condition. When she snuck down to the morgue, she had a sneaking suspicion of what she was going to find. They were harvesting organs. The patients were all lower-income or homeless – prime targets.

Gary Scott, the chief surgeon, nearly caught her prying but instead tried to make an awkward pass at her, sending her running for the hills. Still, she was nervous and knew she needed to find someone who could help her. She could call the police, but she had no evidence at all.

"Reach out," she whispered to herself. Searching the internet, she found a last known address for a Quincy Slater in a small town in Virginia. I mean, how many Quincy Slaters could there be on the East Coast? It appeared that he was working for a motorcycle and automotive shop out of a place called Club Steel. Googling the name, she found the number and called.

"Club Steel, this is Hawk," said the chipper voice.

"Hi, may I speak to Quincy," she said.

"Quincy? Oh, Zulu, yea, he's not feeling well right now. Can I take a message?"

"Yes, can you tell him Gabi called, and I need his help?" she said. She heard the sound outside her apartment door and froze, listening again for the scratching sound.

"Sure. But if you need help, maybe I can do something. Hello?" Gabi hit end on the call and listened more intently. Quietly standing, she looked out the peephole and saw nothing. She carefully opened the door and looked both ways, turning back to shut the door, she noticed the note.

Keep your mouth shut or die

CHAPTER THREE

After another restless night of sleep and dreams of a man hovering above her, a very particular, very specific man. She showered, hoping to wash away the cobweb of thoughts, grabbed her usual plain bagel and coffee, rushing to work.

Gabi entered the hospital the next day, expecting a full slate of surgeries facing her. Instead, she was met by Gary Scott in the hall outside the doctors' lounge. His face was filled with anger and disappointment, and she actually took a step backward, worried for a moment that he would strike her.

"Good morning, Gary. Everything okay?" she asked nervously, trying to step around him to enter the lounge. He blocked her, standing so close she could feel the heat from his body.

"I don't know, Gabi. Is it?" he said sarcastically, looking her up and down with a loathsome glare.

"I don't know, Gary. That's why I'm asking you. You look upset by something." She looked up and down the hallway, trying to find someone to referee this moment, but no one came.

"Come with me," he said, gripping her arm, his fingers digging into her skin as he forcibly pulled her with him.

"Ouch, Gary, you're hurting me. Let me go," she said, wiggling. "I need to put my things in my locker…" He held onto her with more strength and purpose than she thought the slimy doctor possessed. He shoved her into the elevator and pressed the button for the garage basement level where only the chiefs of each department were allowed to park.

"Gary, where are we going. I don't like this. I think we need to get off," she tried to reach for the panel, but he swatted her arm away with a hard slap. Gabi swallowed hard, a feeling of panic rising in her chest. What the hell was happening here? Gary was a narcissistic asshole, but he'd never touched her or made a blatant move on her before.

The elevator stopped, and he shoved her hard, forcing her out the doors. Her foot caught as she tumbled forward, landing on her hands. Immediately, she winced, the strain felt in her wrists.

Damn! I'm a surgeon. I need my hands. I don't need to break a wrist or arm.

"Gary," she called with a shaky voice.

"Shut the fuck up!" he yelled. "You just had to get nosey, didn't you, Gabi? Couldn't keep your freakish eyeballs to yourself."

"Hey," she said, swallowing, "that's uncalled for. I don't make fun of your bald spot on the back of your head."

"Fuck you, Gabi, fuck you! You stupid bitch!" Gary was nearly foaming at the mouth when she finally pushed herself upright, standing in front of him. Another man walked around a large van. His hands covered in leather gloves. He was big, bigger than Gary for sure. Gabi was five-foot-nine and a solid one hundred and fifty pounds, but this man was much bigger than her. She swallowed and stepped back, hoping to hit the button on the elevator again.

"This the bitch?" asked the man.

"Yea, make sure she doesn't talk," said Gary. He walked toward his own brand new Mercedes Benz and took off through the garage.

"Wh-what are you doing?" asked Gabi, backing up. "I don't know why you're doing this. I don't know anything..."

"Shut up, bitch. You won't feel this for long," he sneered, stepping closer. All sorts of scenarios were running through Gabi's mind, but when he swung a big-booted foot at her head, they all were gone. Blistering pain registered in her mind as darkness enveloped her. Her only thoughts were of disappointment at never seeing her dream man again.

Gabi moaned as she attempted to open her eyes. Her vision blurred for a moment, a wave of nausea overtaking her body, and she stilled, trying to regain her equilibrium. She looked at her watch, four hours, four hours since the time she'd walked into the hospital. Now, lying in a pool of blood in her apartment, Gabi moaned trying to get up off her floor. How the fuck did she end up here? The man... the man in the garage. Gary...

Pushing herself up, she leaned against the sofa and moaned, pain radiating across her abdomen and chest. Lifting her scrub shirt, she noticed the purple bruises forming on her side. He'd probably kicked her more than once from the looks of things. She touched her side gently and tried to open her mouth to let out a loud expletive, but the intense pain was more than she could stand.

Fuck! She touched her face and knew immediately that he'd dislocated her jaw.

She pushed up again, this time making it to the sofa, and winced again. Lifting her left pant leg, she noticed that her shin was black and blue, but she didn't think it was broken. Looking down at her hands, she breathed a sigh of relief that her fingers weren't broken. Gabi felt a burning on her legs and pulled up both pant legs, looking down once more to see that the scrub pants were bloody.

She'd been so out of it looking at the bruises she hadn't noticed all the cuts on her legs. Some were deep, some shallow, but all were made by a very sharp blade. Looking down at the pool of blood, she scanned her body once more. Where had all the blood come from? Standing, she limped to the bathroom and saw the large gash on the side of her head.

"Okay," she mumbled to herself, wincing at that one simple word trying to escape her lips. Note to self, don't open your mouth. Time to get out of dodge and find help. Looking around the room, she spotted her purse and her car keys. They must have thought this would look like a robbery if she were found.

She tossed a few articles of clothing in a bag and grabbed her wallet. Pulling on a hoodie, she covered her hair and face and locked the apartment door. Sitting in the driver's seat, she googled Club Steel once more, plugged in the address to her old GPS, and followed the directions.

Please be there; please help me; please remember me.

CHAPTER FOUR

Zulu sat up in his bed, wiping the sweat from his face. He'd lain down to take a quick rest before the party tonight and immediately fell asleep exhausted from the dreams that were haunting him nightly. His ribs were healed, and he was feeling good after the incident with the big Russian, but it was the dream once again depriving him of sleep.

Fifteen years, fifteen years of dreaming of a woman almost angelic leaning over him, whispering words of comfort and love to him. Her hair was a shade of blonde he'd never seen in his life, a silvery-white, her eyes literally glowing down at him like a big spinning replica of the globe, swirling shades of white, gray, green, and blue. She smelled like heaven, and her skin was so soft he instantly hardened. It was as if she were right here. He could feel her. He could smell her.

Every fucking night. Every fucking night for fifteen years. He thought he might seriously be losing his damned mind. It wasn't like he got trashed every weekend and took any warm body home with him. In fact, he rarely dated anyone. He had more than a few one-night stands, but it was always at the girl's place or a hotel room. He didn't live a life conducive to long-term relationships. He was honest and upfront, one night and one night only, and he would leave before the night was over. Always.

He pushed off the bed and turned on his shower, waiting for the steam to rise. Shoving down his sweatpants, he stepped beneath the hot spray and moaned at the way his shoulders instantly relaxed. Looking down, he realized he had another problem, the same one he got after every dream. He was rock, fucking hard. His big cock bouncing in front of him as if taunting him.

"Shit!" he cursed. Reaching for the soap, he cleaned himself first and then let his hand glide up and down his long hard cock. He had more than most and was well aware of it. The guys would razz him in the showers, and the women that were lucky enough to have experienced it always wanted more. Problem for Zulu was they were never the woman he wanted.

Rubbing more furiously, he pictured her face in front of him. That long silvery hair flowing around her shoulders, those eyes glowing back at him, her lips, the feel of her lips.

"Fuuuuuck!" he groaned, relieving himself against the shower wall. He tried to calm his breathing, settle the images in his head. He finally turned off the shower and got himself dressed.

He wasn't a fan of New Year's Eve, but Club Steel always threw a party for its loyal patrons and a few of the townspeople. Tonight, he would show up for a bit, have a drink or two with his buddies, and then return to his room.

Maybe he'd even take off for a few days. Find someplace quiet for him to retreat to and get his head together. Maybe if he just drove, his dreams would lead him to the woman. Maybe.

He walked down the steps through the first of the two steel doors and smiled when he noticed that two of the rooms used by the single guys for 'entertaining' were already closed. He heard the distinct sound of Razor in one and one of the twins in the other, although he couldn't tell the little fuckers apart.

New Year's Eve at the club was a crazy event. A live band played while couples danced and swayed across the floor, filled with champagne or the cocktail of their choice. Most of the guys were seated at one of two tables reserved for the Steel Patriots. Doc wasn't there. He'd surprised Bree with a three-day weekend in Miami, enjoying some well-deserved fun in the sun away from all the chaos.

Whiskey looked up at him as he sat across from his friend and frowned. He knew the big man could see exactly what was wrong with him. Of all the guys in the club, Whiskey knew about the dreams causing his loss of sleep.

"Another dream last night?" asked Whiskey. Zulu looked up at his friend and nodded.

"This afternoon! They're getting more vivid, more intense if that makes sense. It's like I can smell her. I can feel her touching my skin, and then she's gone. I feel like I'm losing my fucking my mind, Whiskey. You know this isn't me, brother!"

"I know, man. I know. You gotta get some relief, brother." Zulu nodded again, looking up to see Ice walking toward him. He had gate duty tonight, and only cars with invitations got into the holiday party.

"What's up, man?" asked Zulu.

"Car at the gate says she needs your help. Says her name is Gabi," said Ice. "She looks fucked up, brother, like she's been hit or something, and she's in a lot of pain."

"Fuck and Doc's not here," said Zulu. "Whiskey? Come with?" Whiskey nodded, kissing his wife Kat on the cheek and telling her he'd be back for her. Zulu walked into the cold night toward the car at the gate. A woman behind the wheel looked up at him. He couldn't see her very well in the dark but knew her face was marked and swollen.

"I'm Zulu," he said, bending at the waist to try and get a better look inside the car. "Can I help you?"

"I... I'm in pain. Please, can you help me? I'm Gabi." Zulu still had no idea who she was, but he let her pull through and then watched as she struggled to stand getting out of the car. Zulu easily lifted her in his arms, the swiftness of it making her groan in pain, and he cursed himself for causing her discomfort. Zulu held her closer, trying to minimize the movement against his body as he walked.

She wasn't heavy at all, her curves fitting perfectly against his hard planes. Walking through the secured gate leading to their private entrance, he took the woman through and upstairs to the medical room. He sure as fuck wished Doc were here, but Whiskey was a crack medic as well.

Lying her down on the table, white-blonde hair spilled from the hoodie, her glowing eyes staring up at him. Everything stood still. No sound could be heard. His ears ringing like a painful echo. He gasped, wavering slightly on his feet. It was her.

"You, you're here. You're the woman," he couldn't finish the sentence. What was he supposed to say? Hi, creepy guy here. I see you in my dreams. He looked up at Whiskey, and the man's eyes grew wide, looking at his face and then down at the woman, and then back up to him.

Her hood slipped off, revealing silvery white-blonde hair, the rosy-red lips full and swollen, and her skin almost ghost-like except for the slight hint of pink on her cheeks, but it was her eyes that had him transfixed. The translucent gray orbs stared back at him like swirling waves in the ocean. He could swear they were literally moving before his own eyes.

Staring into his face, Gabi let out a long, slow sigh of relief. He was here, and he was exactly as she remembered. The problem was, she didn't think he remembered her judging by the look on his face.

"Do you remember me?" she said with a tight mouth, tears filling her eyes.

"I'm trying. I mean, I dream of you sometimes and," she nodded her head with some relief.

"You were in Walter Reed for a bullet to the abdomen that went through and lodged at your spine. I was your attending." The dawn of remembrance started to flow through him. "There was a storm, a hurricane, and most of the staff moved with the patients to higher floors, but you couldn't be moved. I stayed," she winced in pain, sucking in a breath.

"What's wrong? Where are you hurt?" he asked quickly.

"Everywhere," she moaned.

"What do you need me to do?" he said, staring down at her gorgeous eyes. She gripped his forearms and looked from him to Whiskey.

"For starters, I need you to put my jaw back in place, and then after that, I need you to kiss me like you did in the hospital."

Happy fucking New Year

CHAPTER FIVE

Zulu couldn't believe what she'd said. Put her jaw back in place? Was she fucking kidding? Kiss her. Hell yea, he'd do that.

"I'm not a doctor, Gabi," he said, staring down at her. "There's no fucking way I can put your jaw back, honey."

"I know," she moaned, a tear sliding down her cheek. "I can't go to a hospital. You have to... you have to trust me. I'll walk you..." She winced, and he wanted to kill someone for causing his angel pain.

"You'll walk me through it?" he said, finishing her sentence. She nodded slightly and let out a painfully slow breath. "Whiskey? You ever do this?"

"Never, brother. Stitches, ribs, head wounds. I'm your man. This? Fuck no." Gabi reached out and gripped Zulu's big forearm.

"Please, I'll walk you..." she cried. He couldn't stand it as the pools of gray swirling ocean begged him for help, and by damned, he was going to do it.

"What do you need me to do?" he asked.

"Another... another man?" she asked. Whiskey nodded and sent a text downstairs to Gunner. A few minutes later, Gunner stood in the doorway, his jaw moving but no sound coming out.

"What the fuck," he started to ask when Zulu turned and gave him a scowl that had him jumping backwards. "Right. What do you need from me?"

"Quin... Quincy, straddle my thighs," she said, staring up at him. His gaze was a myriad of emotions. Lust, confusion, pain, and desire. All of which she was happy to be a part of later.

"I'm too heavy," he said. She shook her head.

"N-no, just straddle, slight pressure to keep me from moving, give you a better angle," he raised his eyebrows with a slight upturn of his lips and couldn't help but grin. She shook her head, and he nodded, climbing on the table to straddle her thighs. He settled his weight slightly against her thighs but held most of it on his own heels.

"You and you," she said, pointing at Whiskey and Gunner. "Hold my shoulders and arms down, one palm to my forehead. Don't-don't let me move."

"Fuck, woman, you don't ask for much, do you?" said Gunner, wincing at the thought of hurting the poor woman more than she already was. The big gash on her forehead was still bleeding like a bitch, blood dripping down her face and into her hair, the crimson color contrasting to her that angelic blonde. Gunner moved to the other side of the table and stood at her side, one hand holding down her forearm, the other pressed firmly against her shoulder. Whiskey did the same on his side with one big hand pressed on her forehead.

"Like this?" they asked.

"Yes, in a minute, let me show," they nodded, knowing what she was going to say. She needed to show Zulu what to do. Reaching for his hands, she held them in her own. "Hold my face."

"Wh-what?" he asked, staring down at her.

"H-hold my face like you want to kiss me," she said, gazing directly into his eyes. "Like you did that night. Just lay your hands," Whiskey looked at his friend and grinned. His dream wasn't a dream, after all. He and the Angel must have shared a moment that he couldn't remember but was dreaming about for fifteen fucking years.

Zulu placed his huge hands on each side of her face, nearly covering her entire head, holding them gently against her soft skin. She placed her own on top of his, the contrasting skin tone once again sending heat straight to his groin. He couldn't help but feel his cock jump but willed it to go back down. Now was not the time or place to develop a raging hard-on. She moved the hands slightly toward the back of her head, rubbing her hand over his thumbs.

"You can do this, Quin. You can," he nodded at her. "Feel... the mandible... the big bone jutting out?" She ran her fingers over the top of his own, guiding him, and he nodded again. She closed her eyes, a big tear leaking down her face. It made all the men want to kill the bastard who touched her. "When I say three, you'll wrap those big beautiful fingers around it and pull forward, understand?"

"Fuck, Gabi, I'm not sure... what if I break it more?"

"You won't. You'll hear a pop or crack. Stop when you hear that, okay?" He nodded again, and she gripped his hands in her own. "I trust you."

She looked at the two men to her side and nodded as they held her arms and shoulders down.

"I trust you... one... two... three." Zulu gripped the big bone and pulled forward with as much force as he dared. He heard the large pop and a crack followed. He felt the bones slide into place, but what he was unprepared for was the howl of pain coming from Gabi. It was like a wounded animal had crept its way into the room and released the most horrifying sound he'd ever heard.

"Fuck!" he said, jumping off her. Tears streamed down her cheeks as she opened and closed her mouth, crying in pain. "Gabi, I'm sorry, honey. I'm so..." She shook her head.

"No," she said, opening and closing her mouth again, "no, you did it. It will be sore, but at least now I can eat and talk. Thank you, Quincy. Thank you all."

"Zulu. Everyone here calls me Zulu." She nodded, but he could tell she didn't like that name.

"Are you a medic?" she asked Whiskey. He nodded at the woman, mesmerized by her eyes. "You're going to need to cut off my scrub bottoms. They cut into me several times. Some need to be stitched. Others you can just clean and use super glue or whatever you have. The wound on my head needs to be cleaned and stitched as well. I have a mild concussion, but if I don't move too much, I'm okay."

Sweat poured off her face, and Zulu worried that she might be going into shock. He wet a cloth and wiped her forehead, gently wiping at the gash. She smiled up at him, and his stomach nearly bottomed out. Whiskey got busy cutting off her pants, her plain white cotton panties now visible to all three men in the room.

"Shit! What the fuck did they do to you?" Her legs looked like a bad road map of cuts and gashes up and down her calves and thighs. "At least four, probably more need sutures, Angel. I'll clean them and then get started. Do you need something for pain?" he asked.

"St-start an IV... if you have it... saline..." He nodded and indicated to Gunner what to grab from the cabinets. He started the IV and waited for her to tell him when to give the pain meds.

"Let me just... I remember you... I remember everything about you," she said with fresh tears falling from those beautiful orbs. "I need help..."

"I know, Angel," said Zulu. "Let Whiskey get you fixed up, and then we'll talk. For now, I'm just so fucking glad to see you... to know you're real." She smiled and nodded.

"Morphine if you have it," she said to Whiskey. He turned and grabbed the syringe, letting the liquid take effect. "Don't forget you promised to kiss me..."

Zulu swallowed, watching her eyes close. He wanted to see those gorgeous eyes but knew she needed rest and relief from the horrendous pain he knew she was suffering. They heard a tap at the door, and Ice walked inside with a duffel bag and purse.

"Thought the lady might need this. I checked her vehicle, and it was the only thing inside. Looks like she lives outside of Atlanta. I didn't find a phone but found a notebook in the glove box." Ice looked at the sliced-up body of the woman on the table and swallowed. Her white hair was hanging off the side of the table, and he couldn't help but wonder if it was her natural color.

"Thanks, brother. Ice? Would you mind changing the sheets on my bed? She'll need a place to rest where I can watch her." Ice nodded and turned, heading toward Zulu's room.

"She's got at least twenty-five cuts on her legs, brother. The four that are deep were meant to cause pain for sure, the others? The others I think they did for the fun of it. Her jaw will be sore for a few days, but she'll be able to eat, thanks to you. I'll stitch up the head wound first, and then you can clean up her face and hair. Fuck, that hair, it's just like you described from your dreams, and her eyes? Shit, brother – I've never seen eyes like that in my life." He looked at Zulu and indicated he was going to lift her shirt. He winced seeing the purple marks.

"Fucking hell," said Zulu, staring down at the bruises.

"Yea, she might have some bruised or broken ribs. Need to check that later. Gunner? Will you clean the wounds as I stitch?" Gunner nodded as Whiskey got to work. A few minutes later, Kat stood in the doorway and gasped.

"Jesus, what the hell happened?" she said. "You left and didn't come back, so I came to look for you."

"It's okay, honey," said Whiskey, not looking up at her. "She came through the gates looking for Zulu. Don't know much else right now. Just trying to get her comfortable."

"What can I do?" asked Kat, looking from her husband to Zulu.

"Can you make sure Ice is getting my sheets changed? Maybe, ummm, straighten my room a bit? I don't know if she'll be hungry, but I guess see if George can keep some soup or something on the stove."

"I'll take care of it, Zulu. I'll get some water and things placed in the room as well and put a care package in there if she needs it." Zulu nodded at her, giving a pain-filled smile.

"Thank you, Kat."

Almost two hours later, Whiskey finally finished with all the wounds and dressed them. Wrapping her ribs, he folded the sheet around her body and then gently lifted her and took her to his room, laying her carefully on the bed. He grabbed one of his t-shirts and slipped it over her head, so she wouldn't wake in a strange place with nothing on.

"She'll sleep, brother. The morphine will help with that. Once the IV is done, you can probably take it out. I'll check on her first thing in the morning if I don't see you at breakfast." Zulu nodded at his friend as he headed to the door.

"Whiskey?" Whiskey turned toward his friend. "It's her, brother. The woman I've been dreaming about. I'm not crazy. I'm not..."

"I knew you weren't, brother. Happy New Year." Whiskey closed the door, and Zulu lay his big body next to Gabi's. Leaning over her, he gently brushed his lips against hers.

"Happy New Year, Angel."

CHAPTER SIX

Zulu woke to the feeling of a warm leg on top of his own, the shapely soft muscles sending all kinds of thoughts to his head. He opened one eye and looked down to see a long slender hand, neatly trimmed, unpolished nails, laying across his chest. Closing his eyes once more, he sent a silent prayer that this wasn't another fucking dream. Opening them, he looked next to him and breathed a sigh of relief. She was here in his bed, and he was hard as a fucking rock.

Her long silvery hair was laid out next to him, thick and silky, her skin so pale and fragile looking. There were some faint bruises along her jaw, her hands had some minor scrapes and cuts, but it seemed it was her jaw, ribs, and legs that took the majority of the hits.

"Good morning," she said quietly, turning to stare at him, those gorgeous spheres looking directly into his soul.

"Good morning, Angel," he said, smiling at her. "How are you feeling?"

"As expected," she said, leaning toward him. "Thank you, Quincy. Seriously, thank you for everything."

"It's my pleasure, Gabi. I'm sorry I didn't remember you before. I mean, I did remember but didn't think it was real. I... I've dreamed of you... every fucking night for fifteen years. I didn't think you were real. I would see your hair and your eyes. I would feel your lips." He shook his head in disbelief.

"That reminds me," she said, smiling. "You owe me a kiss." He chuckled, leaning towards her.

"I always pay my debts, Angel." He lifted on his elbow, leaning over, gently brushing his lips against hers. He started to pull back when he felt her hand at the back of his neck, holding him there against her luscious mouth. She couldn't open her mouth completely, but she slid her tongue along the seam of his lips, and he groaned.

"Fucking hell, Angel face. You're hurt."

"I know, but I've been dreaming of you for fifteen years as well, dreaming of that kiss. The kiss I judged all others by," she said with a small smile. He looked at her in complete disbelief.

"Wh-what?" She nodded.

"That night of the hurricane, I was glad that it was just you and me in the room. You were the most beautiful man I'd ever seen. When I operated on you, I have to admit that I took a good long look at your body, and it made me blush in all the right ways." He laughed at her and kissed her soft cheek.

"I held your hand and talked to you, even though you were out of it. I knew that you could hear me. The storm got so bad, and I was so scared, so worried that I wouldn't be able to protect you. At one point, at one point, I laid next to you, wishing that it was you keeping me safe. It was dangerous and stupid. I could have injured you, or someone could have come in, but you were so beautiful."

"I was beautiful!?" he said.

"Yes. Quincy, you were larger than life in every respect," she said, blushing. "When I did your surgery, all I could think was I needed to make sure this beautiful man could walk out of this hospital so that I could ask him to take me to dinner. I've never felt so bold with a man in all my life. I lay next to you in that bed, holding your hand, and I simply lost all sense of professionalism. It wasn't doctor and patient. It was simply man and woman. I kissed your jaw, and it was like a fairy tale. You just woke up. You turned and looked at me as if you had been expecting me to be there. You touched my face and then my neck, pulling me closer, and..."

"Kissed you. I kissed you," he said, staring at her. She nodded, and he leaned forward again, kissing her gently. "Gabi."

"Gabrielle, but you can call me Gabi," she said quietly. He nodded.

"Okay, Gabrielle, Angel, I have dreamed of you for fifteen years. Tortured myself thinking you were something making me go crazy. Why did you leave?"

"I didn't," she said, shaking her head. "The storm ended, and we all scrambled to get the patients back in their rooms, assessing the damage to the hospital. My shift ended, and I was off for two days. When I returned, they'd moved you to another room, no longer under my care. Every time I tried to see you, there were men in your room, and I couldn't get in to be alone with you. Then you were transferred out to a rehab hospital and returned to active duty. I've thought about you so much, Quincy. It's completely silly that all I can think about is that one simple kiss we shared."

"It's not silly, and it wasn't simple," he said, running his big fingers down her side. "I've thought of nothing else as well. There's something here, Angel. Something neither of us can ignore, and God knows someone or something was leading us back to one another. We couldn't be more different if we tried. On completely different spectrums of the color wheel." She laughed, shaking her head.

"Yea, well, I'm kind of on the other spectrum with everyone. It doesn't bother me. Does it bother you?" she asked cautiously.

"Bother me? It's fucking hot as all shit! Gabrielle, you do get that your name is a version of Gabriel as in the Angel Gabriel? You look just like an Angel, ethereal, otherworldly. I have never in my life seen anyone who looks like you, and it's fucking amazing."

"No one, no one has ever described me that way," she said quietly. He gently pulled her closer to his own body, molding her against his massive frame.

"Is this okay?" he asked.

"For now," she grinned. "I hope there will be more, so much more. But I know I have to heal a bit first and fix my issue." He smiled at her, kissing her forehead, then her nose, then settling against her lips once more.

"We have all the time in the world, Angel." She stilled then and pushed herself up, leaning against the headboard.

"Wellll..."

CHAPTER SEVEN

Zulu walked into the kitchen with Gabrielle tucked beneath his big arm, and all eyes turned toward them, mouths open, gawking at the interesting couple, but also the fact that there was a woman with Zulu.

"Good morning," she said quietly, staring back at the audience they now had. "I'm Dr. Gabrielle London, Gabi." A few quiet good mornings were heard, and all eyes turned to Zulu. The one man who never brought a woman home.

"Everyone, Gabrielle is an old friend. She removed the bullet that lodged near my spine about fifteen years ago, and we've been seeing each other in our dreams for fifteen years, thinking of one another since then."

"Jesus," said Ghost. "I remember that! We were in Columbia, and you were shot pulling those little boys out of the well. Everyone was freaking out because it had gone through your stomach and lodged at your spine; hell, we weren't even sure we could get you home. The doctors initially said he would never serve again, and you said you knew you would be able to get the bullet out. You did that. You saved his ass!" Zulu nodded and smiled, gripping Gabrielle's hand a little tighter.

"Well, welcome, doc," said George, grinning at the ghostly beauty.

"Hi, Gabi," said Whiskey, coming into the room with Kat. "You feeling okay this morning?"

"Yes, thank you, a little dizzy if I move too fast, a bit stiff and sore but okay, and thank you, all of you, for taking me in," she said. Ghost raised an eyebrow at Zulu as they sat down at the table.

"Gabrielle has a problem that she needs help with. If we can, I'd like to help her as a team. If you choose not to do it, it's cool, but I'll take leave to help her." Zulu looked down at his food and said nothing.

"What the ever-loving fuck?" said Ghost. "We're a team, Zulu. T-e-a-m. That means we work together. If this is important to you, if she's important to you, then we help." Zulu nodded at his friend.

"Gabrielle," said Kat, looking at the woman, "I hope you don't mind, but I have to say you are the most striking woman I've ever seen in my life. Your eyes are incredible, and I would kill to have that hair!"

"That's really kind of you," she said, blushing.

"She's not bullshitting, Angel," said Eagle. "That's some sci-fi fantasy shit there. I mean, you're fucking incredible-looking. I thought you might be wearing contacts, but that's amazing." Eagle heard the low growl emanating from Zulu's chest and grinned at the big man. Zulu was pretty even-keeled, but when you pissed him off, it was probably in your best interest to run the other way.

"It's okay," she said, nudging Zulu. "I have what most doctors would call a deformity in my melanin. I'm not an albino, but I'm probably only a few steps from it. I was born with my hair exactly like it is now. This sort of thick silver-blonde. My eyes are described as translucent, meaning they're almost transparent. Although they are technically gray, I have shades of blue and green that often appear to be swirling. It's really just a trick of the light, lucky me. It doesn't affect my vision, although many doctors have tried to say I shouldn't operate."

As she spoke, Zulu noticed that everyone was leaning closer and closer to Gabrielle as if she were some exhibit at the zoo. He cleared his throat, and they all sat back.

"Sorry, Angel," said Gunner. "I saw those peepers last night and couldn't believe it, but in the daylight, they're pretty amazing."

"Okay," said Ghost, "now that we've all established that Angel eyes has Angel eyes, what can we help you with, Gabrielle."

"I work at South Atlanta General as an emergency room surgeon. A few weeks ago, I started noticing an unusual number of patients coming in that didn't appear to have any real medical issues, but none of them were leaving. They were checked in and then would simply disappear, or at least that's what I thought. They weren't surgical patients. Meaning, they weren't on the surgical rotation or schedule, so there was no need for me to follow up with them."

"You mean not leaving as in permanently assigned to a room?" asked Hawk.

"No, I mean, they came in with no real symptoms written in the charts, but there were no discharge papers. It would usually say 'patient admitted with abdominal pain' or 'patient admitted with broken ulna,' but there was none of that. It was simply a patient chart without a name assigned to a room. I decided to start looking into it. It didn't make any sense at all. I finally found a pattern, everything tying back to our Chief of Surgery. Five nights ago, I found four patients, all admitted. All underwent surgery for various non-described 'issues,' but there was no sign of them anywhere."

"I made the foolish decision to go to the morgue, and there they were. All dead, all missing various organs."

"Fuck, they're harvesting," said Whiskey. Gabrielle nodded.

"I think that's exactly what they're doing. Organs are big money, big business. Although harvesting was once thought to be prevalent, we don't see it that much anymore because it's such a highly skilled thing to tackle. Most of these men and women that I found were underprivileged, homeless, that sort of thing. Two were veterans referred to us from the VA."

"They cut open brothers?" said Razor, almost horrified by the thought. She nodded again, looking at the room of people.

"Sorry, before we continue, can we introduce ourselves. I feel like I only caught a few of the names, and I don't do well not knowing everyone."

"Sure thing, sorry, Angel," said Zulu. "Ghost is our team lead and head honcho around here. You met Whiskey and Gunner last night. Kat is Whiskey's wife. Gracie, that beautiful baby mama, is married to Ghost. Then we have the annoying as shit twins – Eagle and Hawk. Razor, George, Ice, and Axe."

"There are a few more who live on-site," said Gunner, "but this is most of us. Doc and his fiancé, Bree, are on a long weekend together, but they should be back any time now."

"Oh, you do have a doctor here," she said, grinning.

"No, not exactly. He's a PA and a medic, damned fine one too," said Whiskey.

"Got it," she said, nodding. "I forget you guys call your medics doc. Truth be told, most of them are more qualified than some of the doctors I know. I was supposed to be stationed in Afghanistan after my residency, but they wouldn't let me go."

"Let me guess," said Ghost. "They were worried about the hair and eyes?"

"Yep. Not a lot I can do to hide this," she said, waving a hand over herself. "The commanding officers were worried that I wouldn't be able to evade and hide if needed and that my appearance might cause a problem with the natives thinking I was a 'witch' or something. I was disappointed, but it's not the first time I've heard things like that."

"What do you mean, Angel?" asked Zulu.

"I tried to do a mission trip with a group of doctors a few years ago to a little tiny village in South America, and they sent me home. I was freaking out the natives who believed I was the sister of the devil." She shrugged her shoulders and grinned at the grim expressions of the group. "I didn't even know the devil had a sister." A ripple of laughter filled the room, and she smiled at everyone.

"There is no reason in the world why you would want to change your appearance or who you are," said Grace. "Gabrielle, I don't know if anyone has told you, but you're positively stunning. I'm sure you're a marvelous doctor, but, girl, you could be a supermodel with those looks."

"You guys are the nicest people on the planet, thank you," she said, smiling at Grace. "What do we do about the hospital?"

"Not sure yet, Angel eyes," said Ghost. "Let's try to get some background information and see what's happening. We have some friends in the FBI that might be able to tell us if there has been a sudden uptick in desire for organs. Until then, you heal, sleep, and put this big ugly bastard out of his misery."

CHAPTER EIGHT

Zulu walked hand-in-hand beside Gabi, his bear paw enveloping her smaller hand. They moved casually around the property as he pointed to each of the outer buildings, taking her on a tour of the garage, showing her where the new gym and clinic would be built, and then returning to show her the outside of his own home on the property.

"Wait? You live here? I thought you lived in the room we were in this morning," she said, smiling up at him.

"No, Angel, I live in this house, built it from the ground up. We all keep rooms at the club in case of emergencies or like last night when we might be out too late or drinking. I don't drink much, but occasionally I sleep there so we can all be together, especially for holidays or birthdays, things like that."

"Wow, that's amazing! I mean, I know it's challenging sometimes for military guys when they leave service to suddenly be separated from their teams or on their own. This makes so much sense to me," she said, smiling up at him. Zulu couldn't ignore the fact that her skin and hair practically matched the color of the snow. It was utterly mesmerizing.

"Yea, Ghost's father left him the land here and the barn. We added to it, but honestly, it was practically perfect when we moved in. Kat, Whiskey's wife, inherited a shit-ton of money recently from, well, it doesn't matter. She gifted a bunch to expand the garage, build the clinic and the gym, and so much more. We all ride, and the custom bikes that are built have become famous. We have back orders for them."

"Everything here is secure. No one can get in. You noticed the big steel doors?" She nodded, looking up at him again. "No one except those that live on-property walk through those doors. There is a steel wall that separates the club from the living spaces. Connected to that are the gates on either side of the building that prevent outsiders from entering our private space."

"Several of us decided to build homes on the property a few years ago. Doc and Bree have a townhouse further down the road, but they've decided to sell and build on-property as well. It gives us all the sense of community and brotherhood we had while serving."

"It's really amazing, Quincy. I wish I had something like this. Something..."

"Something what, Angel?" he said, turning her in his arms.

"I-I've been alone a long time, Quincy. I'm thirty-eight years old, and I've only had two serious relationships, and they weren't even good relationships. My parents passed away a few years ago, I have no siblings, and honestly, friends are hard to come by when you look like me."

"What the fuck is wrong with the way you look?" he growled.

"See, that's why you're so damned sweet," she grinned. "Not everyone can overlook differences, Quincy. Maybe you can because you already know what it feels like to be the biggest man in the room, or the strongest, or the darkest. You understand what I feel like to be the whitest or have the strangest hair or eyes. Maybe that's why you and I..."

"We're made for each other?" he finished. She blushed, and the hint of pink on her white cheeks was hot as fuck.

"Maybe. I mean, what does it say about us that we've been thinking about one another for fifteen years? I know that I've been thinking of you, and from the sounds of it, you've been thinking of me."

"Angel, I have thought of little else other than you. I honestly didn't think you were real. Thought I was losing my fucking mind. We are different, no doubt, and it's probably part of the attraction. I want to get to know you, Angel. I want to know that beautiful mind that goes with that beautiful face and body," he said, turning her to face him. He lifted a large hand, gently cupping her cheek. He leaned down and kissed her.

"I want you, Quincy," she said against his lips. "I've wanted you for so long." Zulu smiled down at his Angel.

"And is it just my body you want, Angel?" he smiled.

"No. I mean, I want your body. I won't lie about that, but I want the rest of you too. It's awful timing. This mess with the hospital and me, it stinks. But I want to try with you. I think I would regret it until the end of time if I didn't try it with you. I live in Atlanta, and you live here, but..."

"Me too, Angel, me too. We'll figure out the rest later." He pulled her tight against his chest, his lips touching the top of her head, breathing in the scent that invaded his dreams for more than a decade. "You smell so good."

"So do you. Exactly like I remember," she said against his chest. She leaned back to stare up at him, the deep rich dark chocolate of his eyes staring down at her, the reflection of her own light eyes seen in his. She slipped an arm around his massive shoulder and gently pulled him toward her, touching her lips to his, a sigh escaped against his mouth.

Fucking hell, this woman is scorching hot, thought Zulu. Her lips touched his, and he felt the warm breath against his mouth, the taste of her coffee and toothpaste. He was cautious of her still damaged jaw, not wanting to attack her mouth the way he dreamed of. She pressed more firmly into his body, and even through the layers of clothing, he felt her curves melt into him.

"Shit, Angel," he said, pulling back with a heavy breath. "We have to stop, or I'm gonna take you right here." Gabi smiled a wicked smile.

"Would that be so bad?" she asked.

"Bad? No fucking way. Awkward? Hell yes. We're standing in snow with a temperature of twenty-five degrees; my dick is still rock hard, and every fucking last one of my brothers are watching us through the windows." He pointed to the barn residences, the kitchen, and the garage windows, and she waved at the smiling faces watching them. Gabi let out a loud laugh and hugged Zulu again.

"I want to be with you, Angel, but you and me alone. I want it all. I know that seems fucked up and crazy, but I've thought of nothing else for fifteen years."

"Me too," she said, kissing him again. "It's insane, but I had a dream about a year ago that we had a baby, and she was this gorgeous little girl, soft caramel coloring with light brown hair and my eyes." Zulu felt his dick stand at attention. Shit! She was thinking like him.

"That sounds fucking-fantastic, Angel." She kissed him again and then just stood in his arms, her head resting against his massive chest, enjoying the moment of finally being with him, near him. From behind, they both heard the clearing of a voice and turned to see Gunner.

"Sorry, love birds," he said, grinning, "but Ghost wants to see us all in the club. Come when you're, ummm, presentable." Zulu knew that was directed more at him than Gabi, but he growled nevertheless.

"Presentable? Is my hair a mess?" she asked innocently.

"Nope," he said, looking down at her, "but my dick is gonna poke a hole in the wall unless you stand back and let the cold air hit it for a few minutes." Her eyes grew wide, and she stepped back, smiling a lust-filled smile, unable to help herself by looking down. He grimaced, not from embarrassment but from the cold blast of air hitting him where her warm body once stood.

"Oh my," she said, blushing, "ummm, let's meet with your friends, and then I'd like to see your house like really quickly, maybe just one room, maybe..."

"Angel!" he barked. "Stop, or I'll take your fine ass right here. Come on. Let's go see what Ghost has to say, and then you'll see my house."

Gabi smiled to herself. They would definitely see his house, and Zulu might just see that she wasn't as shy as he thought. She had plans for him, big, big plans.

CHAPTER NINE

The huge conference room had a massive hand-hewn, rustic oak table in the center with more than twenty chairs circling it. Against the walls were at least twenty more chairs, all filled with men, some of whom she'd met and others she didn't know yet. There were photos of emblems from the various branches of service on the wall and a few scattered photos of what appeared to be custom-built motorcycles.

"Have a seat, doc," said Ghost. She noticed a tall, lean man looking up at Ghost and realized that he was probably the one they called Doc on a regular basis.

"I assume you're Doc?" she said, smiling at the man. He rose and extended a hand out to greet her.

"Yes, ma'am, although I guess that's going to get confusing, isn't it?" he said, smiling.

"Nope, not at all. You're Doc, not me. Let's just stick with Gabi or Gabrielle," she smiled.

"I prefer Angel eyes," said Ghost, grinning at the woman.

"Just Angel for me," said Hawk. Zulu let a low rumbling growl escape his chest, and Doc laughed, looking back at Whiskey and Gunner.

"It's just like you said. Papa bear has found his Angel," said Doc, laughing. Gabi couldn't help but chuckle at the playful banter of the men in the room. She liked that they so easily included her into their fold and didn't hold back when it came to her and Quincy's relationship.

"You're all assholes," said Zulu with a menacing expression on his face. Gabi squeezed his fingers and leaned over, kissing his cheek. He couldn't help but let his features soften and smiled at her. She nodded at Doc, and he stared for a moment longer than usual.

"They're odd," she said. "My eyes. I know."

"I'm really sorry, Angel, but now I get why they call you that. Between your hair and eyes, you look just like a fucking Angel. I don't think I've ever seen that combination before. Is it a form of albino?" he asked clinically.

"No, I've been tested for it, and it's not that at all. My hair is just this color. Silver-blonde is what it's been labeled. My understanding is women pay a lot of money to get this color, lucky me," she said sarcastically. "My eyes are translucent, gray mostly with some blue and green. Definitely odd, extraordinarily rare, but no optical defect."

It was such a clinical, cold way to discuss herself, thought Zulu. Talking to Doc as if she were discussing a patient, not herself. He hated that she'd learned to refer to herself in that way. He knew a thing or two about people staring at your physical appearance. Often as the biggest man in the room, and usually the darkest, he was looked at as an oddity.

The worst part for him, and he guessed for her as well, was the ridiculous questions. Do you play ball? Did you ever play ball? Have you always been this big? Do you lift weights? Or his favorite, from both men and women, is your cock as big as your foot. That one always made him angry. He suspected that poor Gabi got similar questions on her hair and eyes.

"Okay, if we can get to why Angel is here, other than you, of course, Zulu. I spoke to Ivan, and he connected me with another guy in the FBI. Ted Mathers has been working on a case involving stolen organs for nearly two years."

"Two years?" questioned Gabi.

"Yep, he says that it's like it's a floating hospital or something. The morgues end up with a half dozen to a dozen dead bodies that can't be identified, and then it moves on. There were three hospitals in L.A., one in Sacramento, two in Chicago, two in Detroit, one in Philly, and now this hospital in Atlanta where you came from."

"God, I never dreamed it was so wide-spread," she said, shaking her head. Zulu reached over and grabbed her hand, lacing his big fingers with her own.

"Gabi, you said that these patients were lower-income, homeless, or vets?" asked Whiskey.

"That's right, at least the ones I saw."

"That doesn't make sense," said Doc. "I mean, correct me if I'm wrong, Gabi, but wouldn't organ donors need to be in exceptional health?" She gave a thoughtful expression and then turned toward Doc.

"Yes, for the most part. I mean, if you're in a wreck and your spleen is destroyed, and you die, it doesn't mean we can't use your kidneys or heart. However, if you're a cancer patient or drug user, sometimes even diseases like diabetes would prevent you from being eligible for organ donation."

"But wouldn't homeless people be more likely to be in poor health, alcoholics, drug users?" said the voice at the end of the table. Gabi looked up to see a lean, tall young man with black hair and striking blue eyes. "Sorry, I came in late. I'm Ace." She nodded.

"No, you're right. Those things might prevent it, for sure. But we can't assume because they're homeless or lower-income that they're in bad health." She looked down at her hands and then up at Doc as if speaking telepathically to him. Standing, she moved around the room slowly, looking at each man, then she turned looking at Ghost.

"Does your contact at the FBI have any indication of where these organs are going?" she asked.

"No. That's part of the problem, why?" he said.

"Okay, no one will think I'm psychotic if I just talk while I think, right?"

"No one here will judge you, Angel. We're all a bit on the lopsided part of mental," said Whiskey.

"Alright, hear me out. Organ donation is big business, a multi-billion dollar business in the medical world. Not something I do. I'm a surgeon. I patch and repair. But let's say, for the sake of argument, I am into organ donation. I harvest organs from willing participants, those that sign the little line on the back of their driver's license, but it's not enough. The wait is too long."

"You steal them?" said Hawk.

"Maybe, I mean, obviously they're doing that, although it's not as prevalent as we believed it to be years ago, but what if I was taking organs from undesirable, unwilling donors to place in patients I didn't want to survive? Or maybe they are willing to donate for a price? Maybe to help their families or something."

"Holy mother of God," whispered Doc.

"Exactly. Let's say I find a patient with a liver that's shot to hell. A heart that wouldn't see another six months. Kidneys that function like a ninety-year-old. I then put those organs into my political enemies, rival corporate heads..."

"We need to find out where those organs went," said Ghost. "Ace, can you try to track them?"

"I can try, but since this was all done illegally in the first place, it might be hard."

"Not if you know what you're looking for," said Gabi. "Reverse it. Don't look for who they went to. Look for who died recently as a result of an organ donation gone wrong or organ failure."

"Shit! She's good," said Ace, giving a rare smile to Gabi.

"It's a long shot, but if we can get the medical records of those that died, I can see if I find any irregularities in the transplant. There could be thousands if we expand the search beyond the U.S., but it's worth a try."

"But wouldn't a doctor know if an organ was bad?" asked Gunner.

"They would. I would," she said, "but if you were paying me to ignore that, to intentionally place the organs in the patient even knowing it wouldn't take, then no one would be the wiser. This is like placing a ticking time bomb into the body of whomever I want to destroy. I don't have to poison him or her and wait it out. I can be crueler. I can give them hope that the transplant will work, hope that they will have another twenty or thirty years, and then destroy them. Losing hope, having it like that, and then stealing it away, it's beyond barbaric. Patients wait years sometimes for a transplant. When they get one, they are put on anti-rejection drugs. Imagine taking those drugs, and yet the rejection begins anyway. They don't get a second chance. They're put on the list again, the bottom of the list."

"That's just fucked up," said Hawk. "What if, what if there are kids?"

"I don't know," said Gabi, shaking her head. "I mean, I'd like to believe kids wouldn't be involved, but again if I'm your enemy…"

"I could make you pay through your child," said Zulu. Gabi nodded in his direction.

"Look for patients that have received heart, liver, or lung transplants. Those would be the most likely. There are other kinds, but I don't think they would venture out. Unfortunately, there is no age limit, no way to eliminate males or females, or race. Again, if this is all an illegal front, it won't matter."

"Any other possible scenarios, Angel eyes?" asked Ghost.

"Thousands," she said as groans spread in the room. "Listen, I wish there weren't, but they could be harvesting for use with medical students, selling them on the black market, using them in drugs. I could go on and on, but you get the idea. I'm going with the first devious thought in my head, and yes, I'm disturbed with myself for thinking it."

"You're not disturbed, Angel," said Zulu, staring at her across the room. "You're brilliant, and that can be disturbing at times." She gave him a short nod and a gorgeous smile.

"What do I do? I mean, I need to call the hospital..."

"Nope," said Ace. He looked up to see Zulu glowering at him. "Sorry, I forget to use all my words sometimes. You can't call the hospital. I checked their records this morning. You were removed from the surgical rotation citing a leave of absence due to a family emergency."

"A what? I didn't apply for a leave of absence!"

"No, you didn't, but apparently, your Chief of Surgery, a Gary Scott, approved it and filed it with human resources. It says you have family issues to deal with."

"How-how do you know," Zulu looked at her and gave a quick shake of his head. She looked at Ace and then Ghost and understood. "Right. Don't ask. Okay, so that prick Gary put the leave in for me, assuming that I either died in my apartment or..."

"Or when they went to check on you and discovered you gone, figured you ran, which means they might be looking for you, Angel eyes," said Ghost. "Anyone know about you and the big man? About the funky dreams?" Zulu stared at his team lead and friend. Did Whiskey share that shit with him?

"Not me, brother," said Whiskey quickly.

"We all knew," said Gunner, looking from Zulu to Gabi. "Look, brother, you've had dreams for fifteen years. Half that fucking time, we slept in close quarters and could hear you. The other half of the time, you slept here where the walls aren't exactly thick. We all knew you were having dreams, Zulu. It didn't fucking matter to any of us. You're our brother." Zulu started to speak and then closed his mouth, just nodding at the room.

"To answer your question," said Gabi, "no, no one knows that I've been dreaming about him for fifteen years or that I helped him. If they searched who I operated on, they would find hundreds of patients, including many from Special Forces since I was at Walter Reed. There would be no way to connect him to me. I called the restaurant from my phone, but I'm embarrassed to say it was destroyed at my last gas stop. I dropped it in the ladies' room and stepped on it."

"Did you—"

"Remove the SIM card?" she said, smiling at Ace. "Yes. The only other thing that would have this location in it is my GPS in my car, but it's older, a dashboard model."

"I'll erase it just to be safe," said Ace.

"Okay, Ace, you get busy on tracking down transplant patients who died shortly after their surgery. Once you have some files for her to review, sit with Angel and let us know what you come up with. Gunner? Get to D.C. after the holiday and have a chat with Ted Mathers. See if he'll give us any additional information about what's going on. Angel? Stay close. Don't leave the property unless one of us is with you. If you need anything at all, tell Bree, Grace, or Kat, or send one of the billboard twins to get it."

Gabi couldn't help but smile at the adorable twins seated across from her. They were exceptionally good-looking, young, but good-looking. She could tell they would be fun to hang with but also suspected there was a bit of freak hidden inside them.

The team stood, starting to leave when Gabi stopped them and began speaking again.

"I want to thank you all for helping. Seriously, I don't know what I would have done if you hadn't agreed. I've been alone a long time. I'm not someone who has all of this, brothers, family who I can depend on, who I know will support me. It's amazing what you've created here, and I'm thrilled that you've found this for yourselves. I just wanted to say thank you. That's all."

"No thanks needed, Angel," said Whiskey. "You're part of this fucked-up family now, and I have a feeling we'll be thanking you for giving us back our old friend."

CHAPTER TEN

"Gabrielle?" called Doc as she started to leave. "I understand you sustained some pretty nasty injuries. Why don't you let me take a look just to be sure all is good. I'm sure Whiskey did a great job, but let's be sure, yeah?"

"Yea, thanks," she said, tucking herself beneath Zulu's arm. It was as if she couldn't allow him to be too far away. She needed, craved his touch, and feared if she let him go, he would disappear. They walked back to the medical room, and she propped herself up on the table.

"Okay, let's take a look," he said, brushing back her hair from the gash on her forehead. "Looks nasty, but Whiskey did a good job with the sutures. Any headaches? Blurry vision?" he asked.

"No, not unless I move too quickly. Probably just a mild concussion. I didn't vomit or anything. I don't even know how I sustained the wound. I was knocked unconscious after he kicked me in the jaw."

"He fucking kicked you?" growled Zulu. Gabi, wide-eyed, nodded at him, seeing the anger in his face. It was frightening and yet comforting at the same time. However, she also knew that she didn't ever want to be on the receiving end of that anger.

"Let me see this jaw." Doc placed his hands along the side of her face, his fingers walking lightly around the jaw. "Open as wide as you can." She opened about two-thirds of the normal and winced a bit as she did.

"Sorry, it still hurts a bit."

"Who put it back in place?" he asked.

"Quincy, I mean, Zulu," she blushed.

"You put her jaw back?!" said Doc with surprise. "Jesus, Angel, next time, you might want to choose someone with smaller hands." She shook her head.

"Nope, he was the only one I actually knew, and I trust those hands," she smiled. Doc smiled with her, knowing that the two of them were right for one another.

"Well, he did a fucking bang-up job. It's in place and should heal in time. Don't chew on any steak for a while, stick to softer foods, but other than that, you'll be okay. Let me look at the ribs." She lifted her shirt, and he winced. "Damn, that has to hurt."

"Again, I didn't even realize it until I woke up. I think he kicked me in the side several times, but I was already blacked out. I know it sounds stupid, but I was just glad he didn't break my hands or arms." Zulu raised an eyebrow. "I need to be able to operate."

"Yea, I don't think anything is broken, but it's not for his lack of trying. Did the dickhead, Dr. Scott, do this?" She shook her head.

"No, it was another man I didn't know. Scott forced me into the elevator and took me to the basement garage parking for the department heads. There's hardly ever anyone down there. This man came from behind a van, he was wearing gloves and a dark shirt, but that's all I really remember."

"Did you get a look at his face?" asked Zulu.

"Sort of," she said, shrugging her shoulders. "I mean, I was scared, and I was more focused on Dr. Scott. The other guy was probably six foot. I'm five-nine, so that's about right. Dark hair, brown eyes, average build, although the round-house kick to my jaw was spot on."

"Nothing after that?" asked Doc.

"Nothing. I woke up in my apartment in a pool of blood. It took me a while to sit up, but when I finally did, I was just trying to find where all the blood was coming from. Once I was able to move, I grabbed a few things and ran. Knowing that Quincy was here, this is where I drove to."

"Glad you did, Angel," he said, squeezing her fingers.

"Let me take a look at the leg wounds," said Doc. She slid the leggings down, no embarrassment or shame, and just stared at them. Touching one of the wounds, she smiled.

"Whiskey could get a job giving stitches. These are actually pretty," she said.

"Yea, well, let's not make a habit of getting the pretty stitches, okay, Angel?" said Zulu.

"Okay, big guy," she smiled. Doc looked at both legs, feeling the bruises for any possible breaks since it seemed he attacked her shins.

"You remember none of this?" he asked. She shook her head. "He did quite a number. The shallow cuts are almost like he just randomly poked, not really stabbed. The four big ones were intentional, long, deep, in or near a major muscle. Whiskey did a good job with the sutures, but if you feel like the muscle isn't healing well, we may have to reopen them."

"Do you need any pain meds?" he asked.

"No. Not right now. I'm taking some OTC anti-inflammatories, and that seems to do the trick for now. I probably should start on a round of antibiotics, but I don't think I'll need anything else for the pain. If I need more, I'll come find you," she said, smiling. "You're good, by the way, really good."

"Thanks, Angel, I'll take that compliment all day long. Get some rest and call me if you need anything." He opened one of the cabinets and pulled a bottle of pills. "If you're not allergic, this antibiotic is what I keep on hand. You know the drill. One in the a.m. One in the p.m. Preferably with food."

Doc left the room as she dressed, Zulu's eyes never leaving her. He wanted her so desperately, but seeing her again with all the wounds, he felt like a selfish ass for even thinking about it. When she was done pulling on her boots, she stood and walked toward him, winding her arms around his neck. Gabi placed a soft kiss against his lips and then leaned back.

"I think we should do that house tour you promised," she grinned.

Damn, and here he was trying to be a good guy.

CHAPTER ELEVEN

Zulu's house was nothing like Gabi pictured in her head. She expected something bigger, wider, more rustic, manlier. Instead, there were clean lines, white cupboards and countertops, light gray walls, light gray tile in the bathrooms, and the bed was a huge wrought iron monstrosity. She suspected it was custom built, and Zulu confirmed that he'd had it made for his size.

"It's really beautiful, Quincy. I mean, truly stunning, and the views of the mountain," she just stood shaking her head from side-to-side.

"Do you have a house in Atlanta, or do you live in an apartment?" he asked.

"I live in an apartment. My medical and student loans were suffocating. I'm in a shithole of a place with barely enough room for me, but my loans will be paid off next month, and I can look for something better then." He nodded, not saying what was really on his mind, which was she could just move here with him.

"I suppose I should have asked this sooner," he said, "but you aren't seeing anyone right now, are you? I mean, honestly, I wouldn't want to have to beat the shit out of someone. I'm not, by the way, seeing anyone, that is."

"No need, big man," said Gabi, "I'm single or am I?" She tilted her head with a small smirk, staring at him. Zulu pulled her into him, holding her tightly. He stared down into those hauntingly beautiful eyes. He felt his body react like it did every time he thought of her.

"You are definitely not single, Angel. I'm sorry if I scare you, Gabi, but you're not going anywhere. I can't let you go. I can't let you out of my sight again, not knowing if I could find you ever again. Not after searching for you for fifteen years. I don't know how or when, but when this shit is over, you will be here with me permanently. I can't let it happen any other way."

"You-you searched for me?" she asked.

"I did. Had no fucking clue who or what I was looking for. I scoured social media sites for white-blonde hair and glowing eyes. Found a lot of crack-pot, scary-ass women doing that. I tried to run through every mission I was ever on, every date, every encounter with any woman in the last twenty-five years. I thought maybe it was someone from high school or something."

"Wow, I-I'm so flattered. I can't believe I didn't try to find you sooner. I mean, I knew who you were. I had your name, and I knew that you were a SEAL. I just didn't think you wanted to see me. When you didn't try to reach out at the hospital, I just assumed it meant more to me than to you. I guess, if I'm being honest, I hoped things would turn out like this, this desire we have for one another. I mean, I could have called the police in Atlanta or contacted the FBI myself, but I'd been thinking of you non-stop for months now, and when I found out that you were at least connected to the restaurant, I just couldn't stay away."

"Angel, I'm glad you couldn't stay away. I'm so glad, and I'm damned sure happy you reached out to me and found me so I can help you. I have thought of nothing except you, Angel baby, nothing. You heard the guys, baby. I've dreamt of you every fucking night. I thought I was losing my mind these last few weeks. The dreams were getting more—"

"Intense," she finished.

"Yea, you too?" he said. Gabi nodded, smiling up at him as she wrapped her arms around his waist.

"I couldn't figure out what was going on. I always dreamed of you, but these last few weeks, it was like you were calling to me. I could feel you—"

"Smell you," he said.

"Yes. God, are we both losing our minds?" She looked up at him with those big eyes, searching for the truth, searching to see if he was feeling what she felt.

"No, Angel, I think we're both finding our minds, our souls, our hearts. I can't explain any of this, but I know that we connected on a level that only we understand fifteen years ago. For me, that connection has never been broken."

"Take me to your bedroom, Quincy. Fifteen years is too long." He nodded, lifting her in his arms to carry her to his big bed, her long hair draped over his big bulging arm.

"If I hurt you... tell me." He set her on her feet in the middle of the room, gently letting his fingers glide beneath the big sweater. He pushed it upward and over her head, the pale skin marred by the purple of the bruises, her silver hair hanging freely against her back.

Gabi returned the favor, letting her fingers trail beneath his t-shirt, the feeling of his hot skin against her fingertips, she pulled upward. He bent slightly to help her lift it over his head, and then she stood back, admiring his body. She knew a thing or two about physiques and anatomy, but this man was like a billboard for perfection. The defined pecs led to a rippling band of muscles that were so much more than a six-pack.

Gabi pulled her leggings down, the cotton panties with them, and stepped from them, her bare body exposed completely to him.

Zulu groaned seeing the thin strip of white-blonde hair, her perfectly snowy breasts with the rosy nipples. When she stepped forward and unzipped his pants, he seriously thought he might embarrass himself just by her nearness. He stepped back and shoved his jeans down, carefully standing. He knew that she'd seen him in the hospital, but that was soft. He was anything but soft now.

"Jesus," she whispered. "I'm not sure that's going to fit." He chuckled and pulled her close.

"It'll fit, Angel, because we're made for each other, and if it doesn't fit, well, we'll have a lifetime to practice. I promise I won't hurt you. We'll take it slow. Okay?"

"Yea, I just, I didn't know they came in that size," she said with a sexy grin.

"Let me show you that size only matters when you know what to do with it," he said in his booming bass voice. Lifting her, he gently laid her against his sheets, her body exactly as he'd dreamed. How was that possible? He'd never seen her naked, never seen her body in the hospital, only her face.

He laid to her side, careful not to press his weight against her injured body. Gliding his fingers down her sides, goosebumps rose on her delicate skin, and he bent, kissing one perfect nipple and then the other, while his fingers danced their way inside her tight wet hole. She was so damned perfect, and his big beefy fingers were trying to stretch her as best as he could.

Gabi gripped the back of his neck, holding him against her skin, his lips so hot and wet against her flesh. She was once again struck by the contrast of their flesh, the mirror opposites of the spectrum, so tantalizing, almost taboo. She pulled him upward toward her face and wrapped her mouth over his, savoring the taste of Quincy. He pulled back, staring down into her amazing eyes.

"Angel, I don't know if I can hold on," he said in a husky, sexy voice filled with need and desire.

"Then don't. Please don't," she whispered. He lay back and pulled her toward him.

"Straddle me, Angel baby. Take me as you can, as little or as much. You control this," he said, gritting his teeth. She knew how much self-restraint he was displaying. She nodded, lifting her hips a bit to accommodate his big fingers gliding in and out of her, the sounds of her excitement echoing in the room.

"You're so beautiful, Quincy."

"Angel baby, you're the one. The one I've wanted for so long. The one that I'm keeping." He continued to move his fingers inside her, his big thumb rubbing against her hard little nub, the smell of her desire filling his senses.

"Oh, Oh God, you're going to make me cum with your fingers, Quin… let me…"

"Nope, baby, let go. Get ready for me, Angel. That's it. Explode, baby," he felt her walls tighten around his thick fingers as her body shuddered around him. "That's it, sweet girl."

Gabi gripped his thick, heavy cock, standing it straight up, giving it a few quick strokes to let him know she was about to rock his world. She rose above it, guiding it to her entrance; she slowly lowered, leaning slightly forward toward his chest. Feeling the initial sting and burn of the stretch, she gasped, taking a deep breath.

"Slow, baby," he said through his clenched jaw. He wanted to tell her to drive forward, but he didn't want to hurt her.

"Oh, wow, oh wow, you're way bigger than I thought, than I dreamed. But so, so damned perfect…" she moaned against his lips, her hips driving backward more and more, taking him an inch at a time until she was fully seated against him, her wet pussy soaking his groin as his balls tensed up.

Gabi looked down at where they were joined, her white hair and skin against his thick black curls, the stiff rod moving in and out of her. It was magical.

"Look," she said, smiling, "look how beautiful we are."

"That's right, Angel baby, fucking perfect. I need you, Angel. I need to move, Gabi." She nodded and started rocking back and forth against him, her sweet body molding to his. His hands were gentle, gliding up and down her sides, gently squeezing her breasts but avoiding any of her injuries. He was so lovingly gentle for being so big.

"Quin, Quin, I'm going to cum again..."

"Do it, Angel baby. Do it. I'm dying here, girl..." He felt the exact moment she released on him, his balls nearly crawling up inside him, tight and full, and then it was like a dam burst. Fifteen years of pent-up desire spewing forward, and his growling release echoed in the room. His body shook with the force of his orgasm, the ecstasy etched on both their faces.

Glistening drops of sweat pooled between her breasts, making a river toward her belly button, and he ran a finger up, licking each drop.

"I love you, Quincy. I know that sounds crazy, but I have loved you for so long," she whispered against his chest, his big cock still semi-hard inside her jerked at her words, her desire so like his own.

"I love you too, Angel, so fucking much." She sat up, suddenly aware of something very important, very necessary.

"Uh, we didn't use protection," she said with a half-smirk. "I-I didn't think to ask. I'm not on anything. I'm clean, I promise. I haven't been with anyone in six years." Zulu grinned and pulled her close once again, kissing her face.

"An Angel baby with your eyes. Can't think of anything I want more than that," he said. "I'm clean too, honey."

"Are you, are you sure? I mean, I know I am. I'm madly in love with you even when it was just in my head. I was madly in love with you, but are you sure?"

"I'm sure, Angel. It won't be easy. I get it. People can be cruel, but we'll make it work. You, me, and this baby if we've created one. You can't run me off, not now."

"Quincy, I wasn't worried about what other people would think or say. I couldn't care less, and I know your team doesn't care. But, what about your family, your parents? Siblings? Would they care?"

Zulu was deep in thought for a moment. His mother was dead, but his father was retired, living outside Fresno. He had an older sister who was married and living in Las Vegas with her husband and two kids. His father probably wouldn't give two shits about the color of her skin, just happy that he'd finally settled down with a nice woman and was giving him more grandkids. Ironically, it would be his 'progressive' sister who would make a stink.

"Just my father and my sister, Angel. Dad will love you, but I won't lie. My sister might not be so kind at first. She's always a bit extreme about race. Her husband had an affair with a white woman a few years back, and she believes all white women are out to take the brothers for themselves. She might not be very nice at first, but it won't matter to me. You're mine, Angel. Mine."

She nodded, understanding what he was saying, but still worried that his sister might not like their union. Gabi snuggled a little closer, her cheek rubbing against his big hard chest, the scent of his cologne and soap mixing with sex. He reached down and pulled the comforter up over their bodies.

"That was beautiful, Quincy. Everything I dreamed of."

"Me too, Angel. More than I ever dreamed, to be honest. Can I ask you something? Why won't you call me Zulu? I mean, it doesn't really matter to me, but no one calls me Quincy anymore." He asked, looking down at her.

"I don't know. I guess maybe, well, the Zulu are the largest ethnic tribe in South Africa. The term Zulu was a derogatory term used for a long time with men of color. I suppose that's stuck in my head, and I just feel weird using it." He nodded and smiled against the top of her head.

"That's true, Angel, but they were also fierce warriors with unique fighting styles. They're highly intelligent and resourceful. I'm proud to carry the call sign, although it had nothing to do with Zulu tribes. Zulu is the last letter in the alphabet used to communicate in the military. I was always the last guy in everything. The chow line, a photo, and even on an op, I took the rear because I could see over their heads in front of me and still see danger."

"I'm sorry, Quin, Zulu. I should respect that," she said, kissing his jaw.

"Angel baby, you can call me whatever you want, Zulu, Quincy. I like when you call me Quin. No one has ever called me that. I'll answer to anything you call me, love, anything."

"Yea?" she smiled up to him. Her delicate hand worked its way down his abdomen, gripping the semi-hard cock between her tiny fingers.

"Okay then, my big beefy stud, I need more Quin. I need all of this in every way that you'll give it to me."

"Then take it, Angel baby. It's all yours."

CHAPTER TWELVE

It was nearly seven by the time they made it back to the club and restaurant, joining the rest of the team for dinner. Grace and Kat introduced Gabi to Bree, and the four women immediately connected on everything from fashion to hair and makeup to food to books and their varying educational backgrounds.

The women laughed about Grace's choice of literature but were also curious as to how she was using her newfound knowledge. Grace had a serious addiction to romance novels with hot sex scenes, most of which she shared with Kat and Bree. When she finished with a book, it wasn't the women who wanted it but Hawk.

Bree had a serious love for anything involving chocolate and, during her recent getaway with her fiancée, discovered it had some very interesting uses. The four women laughed about that one begging for details and ideas on how to make their own chocolate sex on a stick.

Kat was still finding her way as a married woman and studying hard for her upcoming bar exam. Their sex was off the charts hot, but she admitted that he was the only one she had to compare since he was her one and only. She also said there were some serious advantages to being with an older man who had been around the block a bit, serious advantages. Whiskey was enjoying her private dances just for him and already thinking about putting a dance studio in their house.

"So, you and the big man?" said Grace, smiling at Gabi.

"Yep, ladies," said Gabi, grinning, "me and the big, big, big man." She couldn't help but laugh at the expressions on the other women's faces. In her entire life, Gabi never had women willing to share intimate thoughts or feelings, and these women had created that safe space for her within just a few days. It was remarkable.

"Damn, I mean, I'm more than happy with what I have, what Whiskey has, but shit, that seems... I don't know," said Kat, giggling.

"He's everything I dreamed of," said Gabi thoughtfully, tears filling her eyes. "I mean that literally. I mean, I knew what he looked like because I operated on him years ago, but I couldn't get him out of my head. It was so unprofessional of me to look at his body in that way, but I couldn't help it. Then when it was just he and I in that room during the hurricane, I, God, I couldn't help it. I kissed him and held his hand. I didn't do anything inappropriate, but I can't lie. I thought about it. Every time I closed my eyes, his body was what I saw. His face, those lips, it was so miserable not being able to reach out and touch him, to have him."

"But you knew who he was, right?" asked Grace.

"I did, but I didn't think he was interested in me. I mean, he was a patient, and I didn't get to see him after the one night of the storm incident. I just figured he wouldn't want someone like me, someone who looks like me."

"Someone who looks like you?" said Bree in surprise. "Gabi, listen to me. I'm a licensed therapist and counselor, so listen to me. Women are notorious for tearing themselves down, picking themselves apart. We're not smart enough. We're not pretty enough, tall enough, thin enough, whatever the fuck we've put in our brains. We cave in to what society tells us is beautiful, how we should look or act or dress. The world says it's okay for men to speak of sex and to lust after multiple women, but it's not okay for women to do the same. The world says we should find one person and be faithful, that if a man is unfaithful or wants to date multiple partners, it's understandable. We all buy into that shit. We all do it."

"All of us?" asked Gabi, almost surprised. Looking at each of the beautiful women in front of her, their beautiful physical traits so different from one another, but most certainly from her own. She worked with a lot of women, doctors and nurses, and most seemed almost overconfident with their appearance or sexuality. She never understood because she was always being pointed out as different.

"All of us," said Grace. "I figured I was too old for Ghost, too damaged. I thought maybe I wasn't tall enough or curvy enough." She rubbed her belly and smiled.

"Yep, I thought I was too fat for Doc, too inexperienced, my hair too red, my skin too fair," said Bree.

"Fair skin I can understand," mumbled Gabi.

"I believed I wasn't worthy of love because of my past," said Kat. "I thought my irrational fears would consume me and that Whiskey wouldn't understand them. I thought if I couldn't dance, I wasn't worth anything. I just didn't see value in myself and was constantly doubting until that big badass Marine wrapped his arms around me." She smiled at the other women looking over at Whiskey.

"They're all very good-looking," said Gabi. "I mean, you can't help but notice how handsome they all are. Well-built, just plain sexy, all of them."

"Oh, honey, we know," laughed Grace.

"Listen, Gabi, your coloring – your hair and eyes – are exceptional in every way. But they're you, honey, you. I wouldn't want to see you any other way. Now, I can see where others might stare or make comments, but ignorance is just that, ignorance. Love is so hard to find, Gabi. True love so very, very hard to find. Despite what the universe tells us, we can fall in love at first sight, and we can have an otherworldly connection with people. I personally believe it doesn't matter at all what the package looks like that it comes in or how you met. Big, small, black, white, blue eyes, brown eyes, it doesn't matter. When love finds you, you grab it and never, never let go. It's just too precious."

Gabi looked around the room at the men casually chatting, their conversations so easy, so comfortable. She spotted Whiskey, her favorite nurse, talking to Doc. Ghost, Ace, and Zulu were talking in an animated fashion about something, laughing at one another. The twins looked as though they were planning something devious. George was joking around with Gunner, Tango, and Razor.

"So, what will it be, Gabi? Are you going to take love by the horns and live it? Or will you run and allow some other woman to put her claws into what's rightfully yours?"

"Yea, that's not happening," she said with an angry expression. "I won't let him go. I can't. I simply can't breathe without him. I know that seems so silly, so fast to all of you, but this has been a long time coming for Quin and I."

"Honey, we don't judge. It was a few months for Ghost and I, but there were extenuating circumstances. Doc and Bree it was just a few weeks, Kat and Whiskey a couple weeks. Love doesn't have a time limit on it. You two have been pining for one another for fifteen years. The fact that you didn't touch, didn't communicate means nothing when it comes to the heart."

"He's just so beautiful," said Gabi, "and damned sexy and soooo damned good in bed." They all giggled.

"Honey, don't you doubt what you bring to the table in this relationship," said Bree. "You're a doctor, a surgeon. You're stunningly, uniquely beautiful. There is no comparison to you, Gabi, none. More than that, you're Zulu's choice. You are the only woman he's ever thought about having a relationship with, the only woman he's ever dreamed of. That alone should mean something to you and let you know how very special you are to him."

Gabi looked back at Zulu, who smiled in her direction, giving her a sexy wink and a smile.

"Jesus, I think my ovaries just exploded," she said. The laughter from the other women could not be contained as they watched the expressions of the men from across the room. Ghost walked toward the table with Zulu, frowning.

"Are ya'll drunk?" he asked.

"Honey, you know I can't drink," said Grace, rubbing her belly. "But no, none of us are drunk. We are hungry, though."

"Here comes the food now," said Zulu, reaching for Gabi's hand. She stood, wrapping her arms around his waist, standing on her toes, she kissed his jaw, then his chin, working her way to his lips, where she lay a soft, sweet kiss with just a hint of her tongue playfully moving along his lips.

"What was that for, Angel baby?" he asked.

"Because I love you, Quin, so very much. No matter what happens with this mess, I love you, and I don't want to spend another night without you." He smiled down at her, kissing the tip of her nose.

"Good news, Angel, you don't have to because I love you too. You're mine, Gabrielle London, mine. I'm never letting you go." He lifted her against his chest and placed a long deep kiss against her lips, only to stop because of the thundering applause by his teammates.

"You're holding up dinner!" yelled Blaze. They both laughed, taking their seats next to the team. It was going to be a long dinner for Gabi because all she could think about was riding Quin again. All. Night. Long.

CHAPTER THIRTEEN

Seated on the other side of Gabi was Gunner, diving into his steak like he hadn't eaten in years. His dark blonde hair and brown eyes made him look boyish, his skin clear and youthful, yet rugged with fine lines around his eyes and mouth. The five-o-clock shadow framing his mouth was sexy, the tiny slivers of gray hair the only indication that he might be over thirty.

If she had to guess, he was probably six-foot-one or two, but a solidly-built two hundred pounds or more. She knew that he was working in the bike shop most of the time right now and would eventually work in the gym but knew little else of him.

"So, Gunner is an unusual name. How did you get your name? Is it a road name or call sign?" she asked. Gunner smiled at the woman next to him.

"Well, Angel eyes, my parents gave it to me." He gave a soft laugh and returned to his steak.

"Wait? You're actually named Gunner?" she said, smiling.

"Yep. Seemed fortuitous that I went into the Marines, right? Got two brothers. One older, one younger named Striker and Hunter. Parents had a wicked sense of humor, and Pops definitely loved his military references."

"That's amazing, Gunner, Striker, and Hunter, very cool. My parents had no rhyme or reason for Gabrielle, just a random name. I actually hated it growing up, which is why everyone called me Gabi or…" Zulu looked down at her and frowned. Gunner turned in his seat to look at her realizing that this was a difficult subject for her.

"Or what, Angel eyes?" asked Gunner.

"Saber like lightsaber. Kids teased me that my eyes looked like lightsabers and when they were feeling particularly cruel, they would joke that if anyone made me angry, my lightsabers could kill them. It was really bad in elementary school when kids' imaginations can't be contained. They all left me pretty much alone." She shook her head at the memory and went back to eating, but Hawk looked across the table, frowning.

"That's just fucking stupid," said the younger man. "I mean, anybody who knows anything about lightsabers knows it's not gray or blue. It's iridescently white. Geez, what a bunch of morons to think those gorgeous peepers are anything close to lightsabers. Can you believe that shit, Eagle?"

"Ignorant fucks," said Eagle. "Seriously, Angel eyes, give us their names, and we'll hunt them down, teach them a lesson about movies and colors." Gabi couldn't help but laugh at the two men. They were positively identical, but their expressions were very different. One grave, one more playful.

"I'm not sure you could even find them anymore, guys, but I do thank you for the sentiment."

"You wound me, Angel eyes," said Hawk. "I can find them and let them know how pathetically wrong they were."

"Don't give them any information, Gabi," said Gunner. "These two crazy bastards would probably high tail it out of here tonight just to get to them. They take their movie references seriously, especially movies about lightsabers." Gabi nodded.

"Thank you, guys, seriously. Give me some time to think about it. I might let you two chase down the mean kids if you let me fix you up with a couple of nurses I know who have a thing for twins."

"Uhhh, no fix-ups, Angel eyes," said Eagle. "That never works out well for us."

She gave them a serious expression, and they both nodded. Their banter, though, had the desired effect. She was already feeling better, and now all she could think about was wrapping her legs around the big man seated to her right.

Looking further down the table, she saw Ace, lots of space granted him on both sides of his chair. She noticed that he had headphones in his ears and wasn't really participating in the conversations.

"Is he okay?" asked Gabi, nodding in his direction.

"Yea, beautiful," said Zulu. "Ace doesn't like to be too close to people, doesn't like to be touched. He's not crazy about a lot of noise either, but he's working on it. That? Just sitting with us at a dinner table is something he hasn't done in the ten years I've known him. Kat is responsible for getting him that far."

"Is he afraid of touch?" she asked.

"No, Angel, something far worse." Gabi swallowed, nodding at the young man. He was really handsome, and she could picture women throwing themselves at him. That dark hair and his electric blue eyes were magical.

"Did you all serve together?" she asked Gunner and Zulu.

"Most," said Zulu. "Ghost, Doc, Whiskey, Gunner, Tango, Razor, and I were all on the same team."

"But you weren't all SEALs?"

"Nope. Special team, Angel, with a mixed bag of crazy. The others we worked with on and off, but all were in the service, some Special Forces like us. Hell, Skull was in the Coast Guard."

"What made you decide to form the club?" she asked.

"Ah, well, that's another story," said Gunner, grinning. "Ghost's father owned this farm and land. He left it all to him, and when we got out, he offered up the place to all of us to remain together. We all loved to ride and figured it might be a way to combine passions. Riding and helping those in need. We built out the garage, do custom cars and bikes now, and it gives us a steady stream of income. We've got the gym being built, which Zulu will run on the MMA and boxing side, and I'll run on the fitness side. The clinic is being built as well. The restaurant is a fully functioning, open to the public restaurant."

"Summer is our busy season," said Zulu, "but if skiing is good, we get big crowds on the weekends in the winter. Menu is simple bar food, burgers, beer, nachos, that type of thing."

"But the food is exceptional, great flavor, good sized portions, and really fresh," she said, taking another bite of her meal.

"Thank you, Angel," said the older man a few seats away.

"You did all this, George?" she asked, raising her eyebrows.

"Yep. Most days, it's just me, maybe one other. Sometimes Gracie helps out. She does a lot of the baking, but we're never so slammed I can't manage. We have a few high school kids who do the cleaning, dishes, that sort of thing. Keeps me young." She smiled at him and laughed.

"I bet it does. Well, my compliments, the food is really exceptional."

"You keep her, big boy, or I'll steal her away, and we both know one night with me she'll leave your ass," said George, winking at the young woman.

"Back off, old man," growled Zulu. The men all chuckled at the banter, and Gabrielle stared at the table of people, realizing just how comfortable they'd all made her feel. Not once did she feel as though their eyes were staring at her own or that they were talking about her. It was family; it was comfort; it was home.

CHAPTER FOURTEEN

Zulu and Gabi felt as though they couldn't get enough of one another. Their bodies were constantly in contact with each other. Hands were joined, limbs intertwined, bodies were touching. Somehow they were always within each other's grasp.

Gabi waited patiently for Ace to get the information they needed to review on the transplant patients, while Gunner and Zulu reviewed the plans for the gym at Zulu's home.

"So, I think if we keep the majority of the weight training equipment here toward the middle of the building and the cardio back toward the big windows, it will keep a big enough separation for the fight area," said Gunner.

"I like that," said Zulu. "This way, the weights are accessible to both sides of the gym, but we keep the rings, bags, all that away from the regular gym-goers."

"If you notice," said Grant, "I've included three sliding glass doors on the west side of the building with a large patio that will serve as an outdoor workout area. You could do rope work, yoga, Pilates, anything out there, and it's covered. The showers will be near the front so people can head right in or out as they like. I've also included an area for merchandise if you decide to create t-shirts, gym bags, that sort of thing."

Grant Zimmerman was the contractor they'd used for all of the houses on the property. Their business for the club was keeping him in business. Two structures, the clinic and the gym, and three houses were currently being built by his company.

"I think it's genius, Grant," said Zulu, "I love it. I actually didn't even think about merchandise. That could be another huge source of revenue if we decide to go in that direction." Gabi set the book down she was reading and moved closer to the table, smiling at the three men.

"If you guys think you'll be a while, I'll start some lunch. I mean, if you're okay with me digging in your kitchen," she said to Quin. He looked up at her with an expression she hadn't seen before. It was part confusion, part hurt, and part anger. He excused himself from the table and wrapped a big arm around her, pulling her into the other room.

"Did I... did I say something wrong?" she said nervously.

"Angel baby, I thought I made this clear, but let my dumb ass start again. This house, you and me? It's permanent, baby, perm-a-nent. What you see here is yours. If you don't like something, change it. If you want more pillows, buy them. If you want new furniture, tell me. You want to break down a wall, let me get Grant right on it. Everything, every fucking thing in this house is yours."

"I'm s-sorry," she said nervously.

"Angel, don't be sorry. I made an assumption that you knew where I was coming from. I'm all kinds of sorry for not being clearer, Gabrielle. This is your home now too, if you want it."

"I do! I absolutely do! I want to be here with you, Quin. I just didn't want to assume." He pulled her into a hug and kissed the top of her head.

"Okay. Settled. OUR house is yours to do with as you wish. If you want to make some lunch, I'd be damned grateful, but you don't have to, baby," he said, kissing her again.

"I want," she smiled. "And Quin? Tell Grant we'll be wanting more bedrooms. Two is not enough for the family I want." Gabi turned and walked down the hall toward the kitchen while Zulu stared at her fine ass wiggling away from him, his mouth wide open. More bedrooms, more family, their family.

Thank fuck!

Thirty minutes later, Gabi set the sandwiches and soup in front of the guys and joined them for lunch. As they talked about the gym, she found herself not only admiring their dedication to the project and how it would be configured to accommodate everyone but also feeling a sense of longing to belong to something as well. It was as if Gunner read her thoughts.

"Thanks for lunch, Angel eyes. All this talk has me thinking, though. Seems to me that you could be helping Doc and Bree in creating the clinic." She looked up at Zulu. His eyes grew big as saucers.

"Damn! I should have thought of that," he said, grinning. "We need a physician on-site, and it makes sense that you could do that. The doctor we were going to use is retiring but took it on as a favor temporarily. What if you ran the clinic, Angel? You and Doc could share duties, and Bree would have her therapy side of the clinic."

"Really? You think he would want me?" she asked excitedly.

"Want you? Baby, I think it's a matter of need you. Fuck yea! Just the team alone would keep you busy with bullet wounds and sutures, but we'd open the clinic to the whole community."

"Let me call Doc," said Gunner, pulling out his phone.

"This is so exciting!" said Gabi. "I mean, I wanted to stay with you, needed to stay with you, but I also want to practice. I can work on getting my license transferred here. My license..."

"What's wrong, Angel?" asked Zulu.

"If-if I try to transfer my license right now, they'll know. They'll know where I am." She leaned against the back of the big sectional sofa, her face looking defeated.

"It will all work out, baby. Let's get this all settled, and then you can work on the license. Nothing is gonna happen in the next few weeks."

"I know, honey," said Gabi, hugging his waist, "but I have bills to pay. I can't just sit here and do nothing, Zulu. I didn't even think. Oh God, what am I going to do? I'm so close to being debt-free, so close," she said with a sob.

"Do you love me, Angel?" he asked looking down at her, rubbing his big hands up and down her arms.

"You know I do," she said with a hiccup.

"Then trust me. I'll take care of whatever you owe right now. When all this is done, you can pay me back by marrying me," he said with a grin.

"Wh-what?"

"You heard me, Angel eyes. I'll pay whatever you owe right now. Then you pay me back by marrying my big ugly ass. I'd say that's fair." Gabi opened and closed her mouth trying to speak. They spoke of being together but not really married. She supposed it seemed like the next step in the process, but still, she didn't want Quin to pay her bills.

"But, but you can't pay my bills, Quin. That's not…"

"Not what? If you say not fair, you're gonna piss me off, Angel. If we were married right now, we would be sharing debt. I love you, Gabrielle. You know that, and I think you know that we were going to end up married one way or another. I'm just saying, let me pay off the loans now, and my payment for that is you agree to be my wife. It's really bribery, but I have no pride at all when it comes to you." She shook her head, tears falling down her cheeks.

"Quin, Quin, that's hardly a chore. I love you. I want to be your wife. How is that payback?"

"You haven't had to cook for me full-time yet," he grinned. "Believe me, baby. I'm the winner in this." She sniffed, laughing a little, and then hugged him again.

"I think I'm the winner, Quin, like lottery winning winner. I love you so much."

"Good thing, baby," he said, kissing her. "Let's finish here, and then we'll get the debts settled."

"Quin? Can you, I mean, do you have?"

"The money?" he finished. She nodded, and he smiled at her. "I'm sure I have that and more beautiful. No worries." She nodded and proceeded to clean the lunch dishes, her heart lighter than it had been in years, maybe ever. Gunner returned to the room and smiled at Gabi.

"I hope you know what you're getting yourself into, Angel eyes. Doc and Bree nearly took my ear off with their screaming. You are now part of the Steel Clinic as the head physician and surgeon. Welcome to the team!"

CHAPTER FIFTEEN

"Did you find her?"

"No, not yet. I thought for sure she was dead when I dumped her in that pathetic apartment. When I didn't see anything in the papers or hear any news from the cops, I went to check. Blood everywhere, just like I left her, but the body is gone along with her keys, bag, and car."

"You stupid fuck! If she tells anyone, we're screwed!" he yelled at the man.

"Don't fucking yell at me! This is your screw-up, not mine!" He said nothing as they walked toward the door of the small office he rented in the industrial complex. He had his own practice, of course, in downtown Atlanta and an office at the hospital. But for matters that were this delicate, he needed private space for the discussions.

He stepped inside the office, and the overpowering scent of body odor and sweat assaulted his nose. Looking at the man seated in the hard-backed plastic chair, he grimaced. They'd have to hose him down for surgery. The older man barely looked up at him, his back hunched over, his gnarled hands curled in his lap.

"Mr. Kaler?"

"Max, just Max, doc," he said, looking up at the man sheepishly.

"Very well, Max. I believe my associate, Karl, has explained to you what the procedure would entail, correct?"

"Uh, yea. He said you would give me five thousand for my family, and all I have to do is give you one of my kidneys, right?" He smiled at the man, trying to show some semblance of empathy.

"That's right, Max. We will give you the cash today. You give it to your family, explain it in any way you like. Tomorrow, you show up at the emergency room asking for me and only me. That's it. Easy as anything. It will take about a week for recovery, but once that's done, you'll be sore but free to leave. No one will know."

The old man nodded and looked down at his dirty feet, one showing through the torn shoe.

"I explained to Karl that I-I used drugs a lot when I was younger. Not so much anymore cuz I can't afford them."

"It's alright, Max," said Gary. "We all have a history. It's fine. We have a whole new procedure now that actually flushes all the toxins from your organs and makes them like brand new." He couldn't believe how gullible these people were. What a cock and bull story.

"Now remember, Max, no one is to know where you got the money, right?" said Karl, squeezing the man's shoulder a little harder than necessary.

"Right," he winced. "Okay, I'll do it. Give me the money, and I'll be there first thing in the morning."

"No need. Karl will pick you up in the morning, Max. We want to make sure you arrive in style. In fact, we've arranged a room for you at the motel next to the hospital for tonight. You'll be able to shower and get a good night's rest. How does that sound?"

"Amazing," he said with relief. "Thank you for doing this. That money is really going to help my two kids. I left because I knew I was making their life worse. This will really help."

"Mmmhmmm," said Gary, staring at a piece of paper. "Okay then, Max. Here's your money. We'll see you in the morning. If you'll wait outside, Karl will get you where you need to be." The old man stood and nodded.

"Thanks again for this." Gary smiled and nodded. As the old man left, he turned, opening the window behind.

"Jesus," he muttered, "we'll need to air this place out for a week to get the stench out. Give him his money and take him where he needs to go to drop it off. Then get him back to the motel and make sure he stays there. Order him some food, but nothing after midnight. I don't need a patient shitting on the table again."

"Got it, boss."

"And Karl? Find that fucking freak!"

CHAPTER SIXTEEN

For a week, Gabi and Zulu worked to find their groove as a couple, although they didn't have to work very hard at it. They seemed as in tune with one another as a couple who'd been together for decades. A week after her stumbling onto club property, she woke in their home wrapped in his arms as always.

Gabi looked at his sleeping face and smiled against his chest. She opened and closed her mouth several times and felt the heat grow in her belly. Leaning against him, she kissed her way down his chest, her hair acting like a sheet of silk, floating over his muscles, tickling his sensitive skin.

Opening her mouth, she let her tongue drag between his pectoral muscles, trailing downward, downward until the rigid, hot cock poked her in the chin. Grinning, she wrapped her lips around him, sucking and licking as she did.

"Fucking good morning to you too, Angel eyes," growled Zulu.

"Don't disturb me," she grinned up at him, "I'm working on a very important operation here." He moaned, almost growling as she sucked him in.

"Baby, your jaw…"

"My jaw is healed, Quin," she said, pulling her hair to one side, the ends tickling his sides. "I want you in my mouth. I want to feel you explode."

"Oh God, Angel baby," Gabi gripped his big cock and lowered her mouth as far as she could, nearly choking on the length of him. He was so big around, she felt the strain on her jaw but ignored it, knowing the end would be worth it. The heat from his skin felt wonderful against her lips, the scent of their lovemaking from the night before hitting her nostrils.

Her ass was sticking straight up in the air, and Zulu wanted desperately to rub his big hands over those magnificent white cheeks, but he couldn't move if he tried.

She reached beneath him and massaged his balls, her finger trailing to the underside, fingering him lightly at his most sensitive spot, and then back up turning the big heavy testicles in her hand, all the while running her tongue up and down his length.

"Angel, you gotta stop," she shook her head, looking at him with those eyes, and he knew he was lost. Never, never in his thirty-nine years had a woman made him cum like this. He felt the tightness in his belly and then directly to his balls. Gripping her hair, he held her in place as he spewed hot cum down the back of her throat.

He half expected her to jump back, spitting the liquid out, but when her lips closed around him, and she swallowed several times, he felt himself get hard once again. Lifting her head, she licked her damn lips, and he knew he was sunk. Shoving her to the mattress, he pushed her legs to her chest and dove between them, his tongue finding what he'd been dreaming of.

"My turn, Angel eyes," he growled. She moaned, her back curving off the bed, reaching for his head as his tongue slid in and out of her hot, wet pussy. Already so turned on by sucking him off, she was squirming with need when his teeth took her hard nub and pulled, then let her go, driving his tongue between her lips.

"Quin, Quin, don't stop…" She jerked at the final flick of his tongue, moaning her release against his lips. Zulu lifted his head and smiled at her from between her thighs. Crawling up the bed, his cock rock-hard once more, he entered her once again, seated completely inside her.

"Fuck, Angel baby, that's the fucking way to wake up in the morning. I need you, girl. I need you again," he growled. Gabi could only nod as his big cock slid in and out of her drenched pussy. The moment for Gabi was when she kissed Quin, tasting herself on his lips. It was the hottest thing she'd ever done with a man.

"Oh God, Quin, tasting me on your lips. Honey, that's so damned hot. Make me cum again, Quin, do it..." She clawed at his back as he reared his head back and growled. Pounding into her, she felt the volcanic liquid spill inside her, her own body shuddering with satisfaction.

Quin lay his head next to hers, kissing her neck, working his way to her mouth once more. Pulling her with him, he rolled and held her tightly, not willing to let go.

"Fuck, baby, that was hot!" Gabi giggled and blushed at herself. She'd never been very bold when it came to sex, and she'd rarely been the one to initiate it. Of course, maybe that was because her previous encounters were all mediocre at best. Quin? Quin was in another realm, like superhero cosmic realm.

"Best. Bar. None," she gasped as his fingers slid between her swollen lips once more.

"I can't get enough, Gabi. It's never enough," he growled. She nodded, already moving against his hand once more, kissing him, desperate to be closer.

"More, more in the shower, now, fuck me in the shower, Quin..."

"Gladly," he said, wrapping her legs around his waist and lifting her from the bed. He turned the water on without even looking, all the while his thick head already inside her channel teasing her. In the shower, he settled her on her feet, turning her to face the wall.

"Bend over, Angel eyes," he said. Gabi bent at the waist, her hair brushing the shower floor. She felt his big palms spread across her ass cheeks and then a sharp slap. She looked over her shoulder, smiling at him, and his eyes darkened with desire and need, slapping the other ass cheek. He slid his big thick cock inside her waiting hole as his big thumb played with the tight hole he'd been dreaming of.

"Do it, baby," she gasped. He happily slid his thumb into her puckered virginal hole. The sounds escaping her mouth nearly made him explode. Her hands were gripping her ankles, her ass blindingly white, angled perfectly for him, the black cock against the pale flesh so erotic.

His feet were wide apart, lowering him to the perfect height as he drove in and out of her.

"Fuuuuckkkk! Fuck!" he growled.

"I'm so full, baby, please, please, Quin," she cried. He pulled out his thumb and put two fingers inside her, and that was all it took. Gabi screamed her release, slapping her ass against his groin, her own fingers rubbing her pussy. Zulu was right with her as a molten hot jet filled her. Stiff and out of breath, he pulled her to stand, leaning her back against his chest.

His big hands cupped her breasts, his lips trailing down her neck. Zulu turned her to face him, kissing her passionately as she ran her hands up and down his body.

"You're so beautiful, Quin. I want you so much it's insane."

"I know, Angel baby. Believe me, I know. It's like we're making up for the last fifteen years." She nodded against his chest, holding him tightly.

"If that didn't make a baby, I don't know what would," she said, smiling up at him.

"Speaking of, I can be a bit old-fashioned on some things, and I was thinking, maybe we need to go ahead and get married. I want our baby to have happily married parents, Gabi. I don't want to wait."

"Is that a proposal?" she said, grinning. He stepped out of the shower, and at first, she thought she'd said something wrong, wanting to cry, but when he returned, kneeling before her, she gasped.

"This is a proposal," he said, holding up the huge diamond and sapphire ring. "Nothing will ever compare to your eyes, Angel, but this ring made me think of you. I love you, Gabrielle London. Always have. Make me the happiest fucking idiot on the planet and marry me?"

"Oh wow, oh God! Yes! Yes, I'll marry you," she cried as he slid the ring onto her finger. "I love you, Quin. I love you, and I hope we have a dozen babies!"

"Uhhh, a dozen?"

"Well, okay, not a dozen. I need some quiet time to have my way with you, morning and night."

"Morning, noon, and night, Angel baby. We'll be working right on-property, so we can walk home at lunch, get happy, and get back to work." She laughed and then looked at him with a serious expression.

"I know I won't, but do you worry you'll get tired of this, of me?" she asked. Zulu turned off the water and wrapped her in a towel, taking her by the hand to the bed.

"Look at me, Gabrielle," he said. "I will never, never in a fucking million years be tired of you, of this, of us. It's all I've ever wanted, my love. This. Is. It." She nodded, tears streaming down her face. "Come on, Angel baby, let's get to breakfast so you can show off that ring. You and the girls can start planning the wedding because I want it done before I put a baby in that belly."

"Thank you, Quin," he gave her a curious look. "Thank you for loving me."

"Never a question of that, Angel eyes."

CHAPTER SEVENTEEN

"I can't believe you guys are getting married!" squealed Grace. "I'm so happy for you. We'll take care of everything, get everything done for you. George and I will take care of the food and the cake. We'll call the minister and have him here right away to walk through the ceremony and the vows."

"Anyone you want invited?" asked Bree.

"No, I mean, I don't have any family at all," said Gabi. "I'm not really friends with anyone that I work with, but I know that Quin, I mean, Zulu has his dad and sister."

"Zulu?" called Bree to the big man laughing with the others. "Are you going to invite your dad and sister to the wedding?"

"Yep," he grinned. "I'm hoping my pops will come. He's been a bit of a recluse the last few years, but I'm gonna cross my fingers that he'll make it out. But not sure of my sister. I'll let you know that a little bit later if that's okay."

"No problem, just trying to plan. Gabi, what about a dress? Do you want to wear white? Formal? Informal? What do you want?"

"I-I don't know. I have to be honest. I never thought of it before. I mean, I never thought I'd get married, so I didn't dream of the perfect wedding like some girls. Given the time frame, I'm going to need something off the rack. Can we go shopping today?" she asked.

"You can go if one of us is with you," said Ghost. "If it's for a wedding dress, you probably don't want the big man, but how about the twins?" Gabi looked at the two men and grinned. They probably thought this was the shittiest duty ever to have to escort her to a bridal boutique.

"I'm in," said Hawk, smiling at Angel eyes.

"Me too, Angel eyes," said Eagle.

"Really?" she said, shocked.

"Really. It could be fun. I mean, all those desperate bridesmaids hanging out in there," Eagle said, wiggling his eyebrows.

"I should have known you'd find a way to make it a pickup market." Zulu gripped the twins' shoulders, and both winced.

"Pickup chicks on your own fucking time. Watch my woman," he growled.

"Yes, sir, sir," grinned Hawk.

"I guess I need someone to walk me down the aisle," she said quietly. She looked up at Quin, who was smiling at her. Something in that smile let her know what she needed to do. "Whiskey?"

"Yea, Angel eyes?" he said, turning toward her giving a kiss to his own wife.

"Whiskey, ummm, what's your real name?" she asked shyly.

"Wade English," he grinned.

"Okay, well, Wade "Whiskey" English, would you walk me down the aisle?" His face paled, and he stood straight up, looking at Zulu and then back at Gabi. "Oh shit! Did I overstep?"

"No, hell no," he said, holding up both hands. "I just never... no one has ever asked me to do anything so special, so, shit! Fuck, Angel eyes, yea, I'll walk you down the aisle, and I'll damned sure make positive this moron treats you right." Kat smiled at her and nodded. Standing, she hugged Whiskey to her, and he pulled back, kissing her forehead. He watched her eyes swirl and shook his head.

"You're a lucky fuck, Zulu. If any other man found her first, any normal man on this planet would see those eyes and take her from you in a heartbeat."

"Not in this lifetime, Marine," he growled, pulling Gabi into his embrace.

"Bite me, SEAL boy. I'm happily married." Zulu laughed and stepped into the hallway with his phone in hand. The first call would be fairly simple, painless, but it would be the second call that would be challenging.

"Hey, Pops! Yea, it's me. I'm good, really good, in fact, Pops. I'm getting married this weekend, and I'd sure like to send you a ticket to come out for the wedding." He listened at his father talking about the weather being bad, and his hips acting up, the gardener not doing his job, and everything but what he'd just asked him.

"Pops, the wedding, will you come?" His father explained that he just didn't like getting out anymore, and Zulu nodded to himself. Since his mother died, his father seemed afraid of his own shadow. At some point, he'd have to go out and see him to see what was wrong, but until then, he'd accept this. "Okay, Pops, no worries. Do you have everything you need? Okay, I'm gonna call Quill and see if she and the family will come. Yep. Love you too, Pops."

"Can't come?" said Gabi from behind him.

"Naw, he's just old, babe, and doesn't want to leave the house anymore." He pulled her to his side as he hit his sister's number. "Hey, Quill, how you doin'?"

Good. Kids are getting big, and we're in the middle of putting a pool in the backyard here. How are you? When are you coming to see us?

"That's what I'm calling for. I'd like to buy the whole family tickets to come out this weekend. I'm getting married," he said, smiling. Gabi could hear the silence on the other end of the phone, and then Quin pulled the phone back, seeing that his sister was trying to face time with him.

Let me see her.

"Quill, don't start your shit. Not everyone is *her*. Gabrielle is the woman I've dreamed of for fifteen years of my life. I love her, and with or without your blessing, I'm going to marry her."

Let me see her.

Gabi took the phone from him and walked to the back porch with it. She finally turned the screen to face her and heard the gasp on the other end. Zulu was embarrassed by his sister's actions but also for himself. He also knew that it had probably hurt Gabi's feelings big time.

While he'd experienced his fair share of racism as a large black male, his sister more than made up for it by hating everyone who was any race except black but particularly white women.

"Hello, Quill. I'm Gabrielle. I'm really happy to meet you. I just want you to know that I'm madly in love with your brother, and I know you're important to him, so I hope we can be friends."

No offense, girl, but we won't ever be friends. Not only did you decide to pick a white girl, Quincy, you chose the whitest girl on the planet!

"Quill! You will not disrespect my fiancée in such a way. I'm sorry your husband cheated on you with a white stripper! But Gabrielle is a surgeon, an intelligent, faithful, beautiful woman, and no matter what you say, she will be my wife. I only hoped you would love me enough to attend the wedding."

I love you enough to NOT attend the wedding, Quincy! I can't believe you would do this! All those good black women out there, all the girls you dated, the girls I know—

"Stop! Enough!" he bellowed. He could see the tears in Gabrielle's eyes, and that was his undoing. "I don't love them. I never loved them, never. I love Gabrielle, and if you're making me choose, I'm sorry to say I choose her."

I'm sorry for that too. Goodbye, Quincy.

"You can't, you can't do this," cried Gabi, her arms wrapped around her own waist, "she's your sister. I can't let you…" Her sobs brought the attention of everyone from the kitchen. George was the first to rush to her side.

"What the hell did you do to her?" he screamed at Zulu.

"I didn't do shit! My fucking sister!" The groans were heard from the men, and Gabi continued to sob against George's t-shirt as the old man rubbed small circles on her back, letting her soak his shirt. She turned at the sounds coming from the group and stilled.

"His sister is…" Ghost searched for the words.

"A racist," said Gunner. Everyone turned to stare at him. "What? She is. She hates white people and more than that, hates white women. I mean, I get it, her shithead husband fucked around with a white stripper, but we're not all bad."

"But, but she's his family. I can't…" Zulu pulled her away from George and hugged her, kissing the top of her head.

"Angel, listen. I haven't seen my sister in ten years, and there is a reason for that. We've never gotten along, never. She disagreed with everything I did in my life. She's my sister, but you're my family, baby. You and these idiots and their beautiful women."

"A-are you sure?" she asked, wiping her tears.

"Never more sure of anything, baby," he said, kissing her. "Now, let's eat, and then the wonder twins can take you and the girls shopping. I gotta marry my woman this weekend!" The cheers from the team were loud, Gabi getting extra hugs from everyone. Ghost and Zulu saw Ace standing at the end of the hallway, nodding in their direction.

"When they get back, she and I should sit down and look at what I've got," he said. "It's not good."

"Of course, it's not."

CHAPTER EIGHTEEN

"What do you mean my father isn't a patient in this hospital?" yelled the woman. "Look again!"

"Ma'am, please keep your voice down. We have no record of a Max Kaler as a patient in this hospital. He was not on the surgery schedule today or any day this week." The surgical coordinator tried to remain calm and tried to keep the woman calm, but screaming wasn't going to do either of them any good.

"Well, I'd like to speak with someone else, please," she said, stomping her foot and turning as if someone would magically appear to answer her questions.

"Of course, just a moment." The woman busied herself with something as a doctor walked up, setting a folder on the desk.

"Here you go, Tammy. I'm done for the day," he said.

"Oh, Dr. Scott, this young woman says her father told her he was a patient here at the hospital, scheduled for surgery today, but I have no record of him as a patient. Ma'am, this is Dr. Gary Scott, our Chief of Surgery."

"Good, then maybe you can tell me why Max Kaler is not a registered patient when he dropped off a substantial amount of cash to me and my brother yesterday with a note saying he would be having surgery here today." Gary froze, the smile on his face fixed and unmovable.

"I'm so sorry to hear that there is confusion," he said empathetically. "Why don't we step into my office where we can talk about this?" She nodded, following him down the long hallway.

"I hate to be such a bitch about this, but we hadn't seen my father in almost seven years, and then yesterday he rolls up to the house in a taxi and hands over an envelope of cash to me and my brother with a note that says he's having surgery here today if we wanted to visit with him."

"That's just awful to hear," he said, shaking his head. "May I ask, is it possible that your father was having a psychotic episode or perhaps a reaction to drugs? Maybe, maybe he's using illegal substances?"

"I-I don't think he's ever had any psychiatric issues, but he was addicted years ago. We thought he was clean, but I don't know." She chewed on her lower lip, suddenly embarrassed that she hadn't thought about the possibility before.

"Well, as Tammy mentioned, we have no patient by that name, and as Chief of Surgery, I would know who was on the schedule today. I'm terribly sorry for any trauma this has caused you," he said, reaching for her hand.

She smiled up at the doctor, noticing for the first time how handsome he was. He had a dazzling smile with boy-next-door fresh, frat-boy good looks. The suit he was wearing was obviously expensive and probably custom-made. She noted the expensive watch on his wrist and, more importantly, no wedding ring.

"No, please, no, I feel foolish for not having thought of it sooner. My father assured us that he was off the drugs, but I suppose a relapse would make sense given that he was homeless. I just wonder now where the cash came from." Gary shrugged apologetically.

"No telling, I'm afraid," he said, flashing a smile at her. "Listen, you've had a rough day, and I'm just getting off from a full, busy day myself. We could both stand to relax a little, I would bet. How about a drink? I mean, if you're not married or anything." *Come little fly said the spider.*

"Sure, I mean, no, I'm not married, and I could definitely use a drink after today."

"Wonderful, why don't we take my car?" He stood and placed a firm hand at her lower back, guiding her toward the door.

"Yea, that sounds great. I took an Uber here. Let me just text my brother and let him know I'll be home later."

Five hours later, he looked at the woman next to him, her lush naked body worn out from the hot sex they'd shared. She'd been more than a little tipsy when he led her from the bar, her tight jeans making him hard as she walked beside him. When they made their way inside the hotel room, she'd pretended to be shy until she wasn't. Stripping off her clothes faster than a two-dollar hooker, she knelt before him, giving him one of the best blow jobs of his life.

He'd taken her in every hole she offered, and when she seemed open to a little rough play, he was more than happy with a little spanking, slapping, tying, and biting. Now she was exhausted, and his dick was aching from the exercise.

Quietly he rinsed off and dressed, then turning, he left her a note simply thanking her for a lovely evening. Hopefully, she would keep her mouth shut. If not, the next time they played would be a little more violent.

CHAPTER NINETEEN

"Hi, Ace." Gabi greeted Ace quietly, standing in the doorway of his office, waiting for his invitation to come in. "Ghost and Zulu said that you wanted to see me about some of the information that you've uncovered."

"Hi, Gabi." Ace greeted Gabi in the same quiet tone, grateful that the woman was already understanding his style. The way in which he spoke wasn't shyness. It was more uncertainty and fear. "Why don't you sit right there, and I'll tell you what I've found." She smiled as he pointed to a chair on the opposite side of the table, nodding to the younger man.

"Ace, if this is uncomfortable for you, I can review the information and get back to you," she said, trying to keep her voice at a low, even register. He looked up, surprised at first, and then let a small grin escape, knowing that his teammates probably told her what his quirks entailed.

"How much do you know?" he asked, shaking his head.

"Nothing really, other than you don't like loud noises or to be touched. I won't touch you, I promise. But because I'm an insatiably curious doctor, do you have autism?" she asked. Ace completely took her by surprise when he let out a loud, rumbling laugh, his pristine white teeth gleaming from between his full lips and that sexy as shit five-o-clock shadow.

"I'm sorry, Gabi, I'm not laughing at you, but that's such a clinical approach, and it's the first time anyone has ever asked me that." His smile lessened, and he looked down at this laptop and then back up. "No. I'm not autistic. I was abused as a child, Gabi. Held behind bars and taunted, touched by my foster parents and other adults. I've never done well with touching or noise since then."

"I'm so sorry, Ace. Please accept my apologies for asking. I won't bring it up again," she said sympathetically.

"No, no worries at all, you didn't know. Honestly, I'm finding the more people I talk to about it, the more comfortable I become around people, sort of ironic. Kat, Kat has a fear of darkness and closed spaces as well. We sort of bonded over that, and I've been trying to venture out a little each week."

"Like dinner the other night with the headphones?" she asked, smiling.

"Yea. That was Bree's suggestion, and I have to say it worked pretty well for me. I enjoyed sitting with my teammates to eat, but the noise level often gets to me." Gabi just nodded, not wanting to pry any more than he was prepared for. "Okay, let's take a look at what I've found. So far, I have about forty people who have received transplants in the last year that died. In all of the cases, transplant-related illnesses or rejection were cited as cause of death."

"Okay," she said, nodding as he pushed the files toward her. "That's a lot. Way more than I thought there would be, honestly."

"Well, I started with the cities the feds told us they had their suspicions about. From there, I just ventured further out." Gabi nodded, letting out a long, slow breath. It was going to take her hours to scour through the information.

"Alright, coffee, my good man, and I'll get to work," she said, grinning at him. He nodded, smiling back at her as he left to retrieve coffee and some sandwiches to tide them over. The amount of data was overwhelming, but what was most prevalent for Gabi was that there were no donor names cited. No records of where or how the organ was received. Gabi wasn't even sure how long she'd been sitting there when Zulu came into the room.

"You trying to hold my woman hostage?" he joked with Ace. Normally, the man would look confused at a joke sent his way. Today, he grinned and shook his head.

"She wouldn't get up," he said, jerking his head toward Gabi, who was still buried in the folder. "I tried to get her to stop for lunch and then dinner, but she seems engrossed." Ace turned back to his faithful computers, leaving Zulu to deal with Gabi.

"Baby? Angel eyes?" he called again. Finally, he sat next to her, turned her chair, and gripped her face kissing her fiercely. "Baby girl, look at me."

"There's so many," she whispered. "All of them, all of them died from complications related to the transplant."

"Is that abnormal?" he asked.

"Y-yes. I mean, a percentage certainly could have had problems, but this many? No way. I need to see the pathology reports, autopsies, anything that we can get on them. I won't know what state the organ was in without that."

"Very few had autopsies," said Ace.

"That seems odd," she frowned. "I mean, it's fairly standard procedure, particularly for people of this stature."

"What do you mean?" said a voice in the doorway. Gabi turned to see Gunner, Ghost, and Whiskey standing at the door. They all looked at Ace, who normally would feel this many people in his space were far too many. He just nodded.

"I mean, one of these people was a high-profile corporate head. Two more were wives of prominent politicians. Three were all from the same family in Greece. Again, my instincts would tell me political issues or crime. I just don't know." She looked exhausted both mentally and physically. Zulu didn't like it one damned bit. "The other thing is that none of the donors are listed or the circumstances surrounding the donor organ. That's not only odd; it's unethical. The donor name might be kept from the receiver, but it would be listed or at the very least how they came by the organ noted. There's something else. Something I'm sure I'm missing."

"Come on, baby," he said, pulling her to her feet. "Let's get some food in you and relax for the rest of the evening. You and Ace can hit this again tomorrow." She nodded as Zulu pulled her from the room, but before leaving, she turned back to Ace, walking slowly toward him.

"You've been so kind to me today, letting me share your workspace. I know, I mean, I was just wondering can I hug you or shake your hand?" she asked. Ace looked over her shoulder toward Zulu, who had a strange grin on his face. At six-feet-one, he was smaller than some of the other guys but kept in shape by running and swimming. Things he could do alone, his long, lean muscles making him look wiry instead of muscular like Zulu.

"I-I'd like to try a hug, Gabi," he said quietly. "Partly because I've never hugged anyone other than my adoptive father, and partly because I know hugging you will make Zulu mad." He gave a sly grin and stood from this desk.

She moved slowly toward him, stopping just a few inches away. She wanted him to make the first move, and when he awkwardly spread his arms, she stepped into them and gently laid her hands over his shoulders.

"Thank you for being such a wonderful man," she said softly, so only he could hear. It only lasted about ten seconds, but Gabi knew it was a victory, and more importantly, so did Ace.

CHAPTER TWENTY

"There she is!" said Grace. "We've been wondering where you went off to after shopping this morning."

"Oh, sorry, ladies," she said to Grace, Bree, and Kat. "I was holed up with Ace trying to look through some of the files we found."

"Rough day, honey?" asked Bree. The other woman reached out and pushed back a long strand of hair from her face, smiling at her.

"Yea, I mean, I just don't even know exactly what I'm trying to find. It seems pretty obvious what they're doing, but I suppose they need something solid to connect it all together." Bree nodded and handed her a glass of wine.

"Well, no more business tonight. Enjoy the meal and the wine. Let's talk wedding!" she said, smiling.

"Speaking of," said Gabi, eyeing the other woman, "why aren't you and Doc married yet? I mean, it's clear that everything happens at the speed of sound around here, so why are you two still unmarried?"

"Oh, oh well, we got engaged before Christmas, really between Thanksgiving and Christmas, but we didn't set a date yet. I don't know. I guess neither of us is in any hurry."

"But you do want to get married soon, right?" asked Gabi.

"Yea, I mean, yea, of course," said Bree nervously. "I mean, we want to start a family, and neither of us is getting any younger. I've been focused on my career and then with the building of the clinic. I don't know. It's just that Doc and I haven't talked about it, to be honest."

"Well, I think it would be amazing if you two got married with Quin and I this weekend," said Gabi, smiling at her new friend.

"What?! No, no, I mean, it's your day, and we haven't…"

"We haven't what?" asked Doc, taking the seat beside her as Zulu sat next to Gabi.

"Talked about a wedding date," said Grace, grinning at her friend.

"I've already said any time you're ready, baby, is when we'll do it," said Doc casually. "The house construction is in full swing. We'll be moving on-property within a few months. I know I'd damned sure like to be married before then, and we both want to start a family soon. I know I'm not getting any younger, that's for sure."

"Good!" said Gabi. "Then let's make it a double wedding this weekend." Doc looked up at Gabi, shocked that she would suggest it, and then looked back to Zulu, who nodded.

"What do you say, baby? Will you marry me this weekend?" Bree looked at Doc and started to cry, nodding her head.

"Yes, yes, I will," she said, kissing him. "Thank you, Gabi, Zulu. Are you sure?"

"Never more sure of anything in my life," said Gabi. "I hate people staring at me. I don't like being the center of attention, so this is a sure-fire way that you'll get some of the staring along with me." The two women hugged while Zulu and Doc simply nodded at one another.

"Glad to head toward my eternal happiness with a brother," said Zulu with a fist bump at Doc.

"I agree," he said, laughing. "Gabi? Ace said you had a rough day with all the files. Anything I can help you with?"

"I'd sure appreciate a second set of eyes on the files, Doc. I've looked at about a third of them so far, and the only thing I can find in common is that there is no indication of where the organs have come from or how they were retrieved, and all the recipients died of complications from the anti-rejection drugs or the surgery itself. At least, that's what the files are saying."

"That definitely seems odd. I didn't have a lot of occasion to be around transplants as a medic, but I damned sure know enough to be dangerous. Where do you think they're getting the organs? I mean, you said there were some bodies in the morgue with no identification." Gabi nodded her head thoughtfully.

"You know what?"

"What are you thinking, beautiful?" asked Zulu.

"Something else we need to check. Missing persons, John or Jane Does. If they're doing what I think, taking organs from homeless, drug users, that sort of thing, somewhere there is going to be a record of a body found or not claimed within a morgue or a police report of a missing person." She looked at Ghost, Doc, and Zulu, and they all nodded thoughtfully.

"Definitely something we can look into as well," said Ghost.

"What about the VA?" asked Gabi. "I mean, if some of these guys were veterans who were homeless or in a bad way, wouldn't the VA have record of patients who hadn't returned or disappeared?"

"It's a good thought," said Doc, "but keep in mind, Angel eyes, that the VA is overwhelmed on a good day. I'd be shocked if any one actually gave a shit about a veteran missing, but it's worth a look."

"Alright! Enough work talk," yelled George. "I've worked hard on dinner tonight, and I don't want anything ruining my creation. Angel eyes told me her favorite comfort foods, and lord knows she's gonna need some comfort living with this big asshole." He jerked his head toward Zulu, who could only shake his head good-naturedly.

"George, you didn't!" she clapped her hands excitedly.

"I did, Angel. Macaroni and cheese with bacon, pork chops, collard greens, and bread pudding with bourbon caramel sauce for dessert."

"Oh, George," she said with a sniffle as she stood to hug the older man, "thank you so much, George. Thank you for making me feel at home, feel loved."

"My pleasure, Angel eyes. We love you, and I'm sure glad you're takin' this idiot off our hands, but good luck with feedin' him." The whole table laughed as conversations picked up again.

"How you doin', baby?" asked Zulu, leaning over to kiss Gabi.

"I'm doing great, my sexy, handsome, warrior, soon-to-be husband. I'm so in love with you, Quin, and I'm loving your, our friends and family."

"Ohhh, sexy and handsome, am I? Well, just wait until later when I show you just what I think of you and that beautiful body, baby," he growled in her ear, gripping her thigh with his big hand. She giggled and leaned closer. "Just for my own peace of mind, Angel eyes. Do you cook?" Gabi tilted her head back in a roaring laugh.

"Yes, my love. Yes, I cook, and I can't wait to cook our first big meal together in our home as husband and wife."

"Damn!" He shifted in his seat, adjusting his aching cock against his jeans. "That sounds amazing, Angel eyes. What do you say we take dessert back to the house?" She looked around the room at their friends chatting and eating and smiled.

"Race you to the caramel sauce."

CHAPTER TWENTY-ONE

"We have a problem," said Karl, walking into his office without knocking. Forget the not knocking. He wasn't supposed to be at the hospital at all. His job was to find their marks, get them to agree to the surgery, and then dispose of the bodies when the time came. He didn't need him thinking. As the surgeon, he was the brains of this operation, although his boss would disagree.

"I've asked you before not to come to my place of employment," said Gary. "You know that if you're seen here too frequently, it will raise eyebrows."

"Yea, well, we might have more than a few eyebrows raised if you don't fucking listen to me!"

"Don't you dare speak to me that way! I'm a gifted surgeon. I'm the one with the brains in this operation, not you. You would do well to remember you were hired solely as the muscle of this team. That. Is. It."

"And you would do well to remember that I can bury you if I should choose. I have enough money to find a little place off the grid and live comfortably while I make your life a living hell. So, get that stick out of your ass and stop thinking that you're God's gift to women and surgery because you're nothing but a pompous piece of shit who happens to know how to dice up a human body."

He watched the big beefy man, anger seething beneath his skin. How dare he question his abilities or gifts? He controlled this operation, not some muscle head. He could walk away at any time. *Yea, right.*

"Fine, Karl, what's this problem we have?" he said through clenched teeth.

"Two separate families have filed missing persons' reports. One was from that woman in Sacramento. She was a hooker and drug user, really skinny…"

"Yea, yea, I remember her. I thought she said she didn't have any family? Didn't you check her out?" he accused.

"I did check her out! She gave us her maiden name, not her married name. Turns out she was still legally married with three kids at home. That bitch looked fifty, and she was only thirty-seven. Husband went to the police and filed the report."

"So what? We got rid of her body, right?" asked Gary.

"Yea, we got rid of the body, but…"

"But?"

"But they found it. We dumped where we always dump, but that asshole we were working with didn't cremate the bodies like we asked. He stacked them in an old tractor-trailer in a junkyard."

"What an idiot! Didn't he think the smell and the flies would attract attention? Did you kill him?" asked Gary.

"No, I didn't kill him! He's in Sacramento. I had things you needed done here. That woman you fucked the other night didn't let it rest. She filed a missing person's on her old man as well. That body is still in the morgue, along with the other four. We have to get them taken care of immediately."

"Then get them taken care of! Clean everything, make sure there isn't one speck of evidence left. How fucking hard is this?"

"You think it's simple to just get rid of a bunch of bodies missing their internal organs?" asked the man sarcastically. "Then, by all means, you do it. You haul them out in the middle of the night and take them to some backstreet funeral director willing to get paid under the table. You figure out the logistics of that and let me know your plan, you prick!"

He wanted to scream at the other man, to call him all the names that were swirling in his head, but he didn't dare. He needed him. At least until he could find his replacement.

"Fine. Get rid of the bodies as quickly as you can. What about Gabrielle London? Any idea where she is?"

"No. The trace on her phone didn't work. She's either destroyed it or turned it off. No one has seen her. She has no family and certainly no friends with those fucked-up features." He nodded, although in truth, her features were odd in a hot way.

"Okay, keep trying." He stood from behind the desk, grabbing his winter coat.

"Where are you going?"

"I'm going to pay a visit to my little fuck buddy and see if I can quiet her permanently."

CHAPTER TWENTY-TWO

By the time Doc and Gabi were seated at the table again the next morning, Ace had another fifty folders waiting for them to review.

"Ace? Were you up all night doing this?" she asked with concern for the young man.

"Don't worry, Angel eyes," he said, grinning at her, "I got plenty of sleep. Once I got started and knew what I was looking for, the information just sort of came in."

"Can you search for something else as well?" she asked shyly.

"I can search for anything," he said confidently.

"We'd like to check missing person's reports in the cities where we know some of these cases have occurred," said Doc.

"That's easy. I started looking into those last night. In fact, one came from Atlanta yesterday. A woman by the name of Abby Kaler reported her father, Max Kaler, missing. Seems her father has been estranged from her and her brother for almost seven years. He came by their home about a week ago with an envelope full of cash and a note saying he was having surgery at South Atlanta General."

"Oh God," whispered Gabi.

"Yea, she went by the hospital the next day to see her father and was told that he wasn't there and wasn't on the schedule."

"Wh-who did she speak with?" asked Gabi, taking her seat.

"She initially spoke with a nurse, Tammy Johnston. When she couldn't help, she was referred to a Dr. Gary Scott." Ace stopped, watching Gabi's features pale, her eyes glowing more, her skin less.

"Gabi?" asked Doc. "Get Zulu." Doc looked at Ace and watched as the young man moved faster than he'd ever seen running down the hall.

"Gabi, look at me," said Doc. He checked her pupils and pulse, then poured her a glass of water, forcing her to take a drink.

"It's him. Dr. Scott is the one who attacked me," she whispered.

"Baby? Angel?" Zulu came running down the hall yelling. "Angel?"

"It's okay. I mean, I knew it was him. It's just hearing it confirmed by Ace. Gary Scott is behind all of this. I worked with that man every day for the last year, performed surgeries next to him, watched him interact with patients, and never once would have suspected anything so heinous. I need to go to Atlanta and speak to this woman, Max Kaler's daughter."

"No fucking way," said Zulu, folding his massive arms across his chest.

"Quin, Zulu, listen to me. You could go with me. Nothing will happen to me with you there. I need to get back inside the hospital and find evidence to help this case. This woman knows things. Things she probably doesn't even see in front of her. I need to be able to stop running and stop being scared," Zulu shook his head from side to side.

"Zulu, brother, she's making some sense. I can head to the one in Sacramento and talk to that family member. You two can head to Atlanta. It will be good. She's right, you won't let anything happen to her. We could even send Gunner with you."

"Yea," she said, smiling. "Plus, we could get into my apartment and get my things. Close everything up. I won't be going back there. We both know that." That seemed to strike a chord with him as he looked down at her. She was planning on moving everything here.

"I can't lose you, not again," he whispered against her ear, pulling her into the warmth of his own body.

"You won't. It's like Doc said, we can bring Gunner with us, and maybe even the twins," she grinned. "I think they're like annoying identical little brothers, and besides, I still think I have a nurse or two to introduce them to."

"Being beautiful and charming isn't going to make me change my mind, Angel," he growled.

"I'm not trying to be those things, honey. I love you, Quin. I won't do anything to jeopardize our life together. I do, however, need to try and find something that will help bring Gary Scott down and allow me to live a normal life inside and outside of these gates."

Zulu looked around the room at Ace and Doc and then back toward the door where Ghost was now leaning against the frame, his long hair and beard peppered with more silver than he remembered. It seemed they were all aging quickly, and he couldn't help but think it had a lot to do with worrying over their women.

"Alright, baby, we go to Atlanta *after* the wedding. Gunner, Hawk, and Eagle will come with us. Doc? Don't go alone. Take..."

"I'll go," said Ace, standing at his desk. Ghost and Zulu opened their mouths, but no sound came out. "I'll go. I need to go. I need to prove to myself that I can do this. I-I need to venture out of this space, my safe space."

"Are you sure, brother?" asked Ghost.

"Yea, I mean, Doc will be with me, and he will know what to do if I..." he shrugged his shoulders and looked down at his computer again. "I need to do this, Ghost. I owe it to my father."

"Okay. Doc and Ace to Sacramento. Zulu, Angel eyes, Hawk, Gunner, and Eagle to Atlanta. Everyone comes home. Everyone."

CHAPTER TWENTY-THREE

Gabrielle looked at herself in the mirror, opening and closing her eyes several times just to be sure it was real. She never spent much time examining her appearance. When you learn that your features are vastly different from those around you, you tend to avoid looking in the mirror as it only reminds you of that fact. She rarely wore makeup and most days was dressed only in scrubs or jeans and t-shirts, so what did she have to look at?

Now, seeing herself in the full-length mirror, she wished she could tell her twelve-year-old self that this would happen. Her life would have been infinitely easier. Bree, Kat, and Grace stood behind her, tears filling their eyes as well.

Bree chose a simple white slip dress that showed her voluptuous curves, the fabric hugging those sexy curves, her breasts stretching the fabric, her coppery curls twisted atop her head with small flowers and pearls woven in the tendrils. She asked George to walk her down the aisle and knew the older man would be crying every step with her.

"Gabi," said Grace breathlessly, "honey, you look so beautiful." Gabi chose a satin gown with an overlay of tulle in the softest, palest shades of iridescent gray. The girl in the shop took one look at her eyes and immediately pulled the gown, assuring her there was no other option for her. She'd been right. The dress hugged her curves, the deep v-neck displaying the perfectly round white globes that Zulu loved so much. The drop waist flared out, the tulle shimmering in the light.

Her hair was twisted in a lose braid with baby's breath wound throughout. At her neck was a wedding gift from Zulu, a strand of pearls with a diamond and sapphire pendant.

"I feel like a princess," she said, smiling at the other women.

"You look like a princess," said Kat. "You two look like those princesses from the snow movie." The women laughed, and Gabi nodded, staring at her reflection and then back to Bree. They did look like the snow queen and her sister. There was a soft tap on the door, and then George and Whiskey entered.

"Wow!" said George, laying his big hand against his heart. He was already shedding a tear looking at the two women. It reminded him of his Mags. All dressed up on their wedding day looking so beautiful and perfect. Damn, he missed her.

"Yea, fucking wow-wow," said Whiskey. "You ladies look beautiful. I know a couple of brothers who are going to lose their shit when they see you two."

"Okay, we'll go downstairs now," said Grace. "You both really do look beautiful." Kat kissed her husband's cheek and followed Grace down the stairs.

"Are you ladies ready?" asked George. "It's not too late to change your mind. I mean, I'm still available and all."

"No changing my mind, George. I'm as ready as I'll ever be," said Bree, taking his elbow. Whiskey offered his arm to Gabi, and they started to follow the couple when she pulled back.

"Whiskey? I-I just want to thank you for this, for being here for me. I mean, I know we only met a few weeks ago, but, well, I never thought I would get married, and when my father died, it was almost like it didn't matter anymore. This means more to me than you could ever imagine."

"It's my honor, Angel eyes. Zulu is my brother in every sense of the word. I would take a bullet for him if he needed it. So, this? Walking this stunning, ethereal beauty down the aisle so she can commit her life to him? This is easy. Crazy on your part," he said, winking, "but easy."

She laughed, wiping her tears as they headed downstairs.

Neither Bree nor Gabi wanted the traditional wedding march, so instead, both agreed on the song "I Love the Way You Love Me" by John Michael Montgomery. Both women felt it expressed how they felt about their men. Doc and Zulu stood side-by-side, tears in their eyes when they saw their brides.

Bree came first with George holding tight to the young woman. When he handed her off, he gave a stare to Doc that came with a warning. Fuck with her,; you fuck with me. When Whiskey walked slowly with Gabi, Zulu nearly fainted, swaying on his feet. Ghost leaned over and whispered.

"Don't faint, dickhead. I won't be able to pick your big ass up."

The image walking toward him was identical to every image from his dreams for more than a decade. He could smell her fragrance, see her glowing, swirling eyes, and feel the silkiness of her skin. But it was the dress that took his breath away, the body-hugging, curve-revealing dress that made his dick ache.

Zulu and Doc were dressed in black dress pants and white dress shirts. No ties. No jackets. Ironically, it had been Bree and Gabi that set the dress code. They wanted the men to be comfortable, not confined.

"Welcome, everyone! It's my honor to perform this double ceremony today," said the minister. "I have married Whiskey and Katarina as well as Eric and Grace. It gives me great pleasure today to join together Quincy and Gabrielle and Jack and Aubrey." The minister continued to speak to both couples, speaking of love and partnership, patience, and kindness. Gabi didn't think she needed any lectures on those subjects. She'd loved this man for more than a decade. Her patience had been infinite in waiting for him.

When the final blessings were given, the rings exchanged, and the kisses delivered, they were announced as married, and the room exploded with applause. Bree and Doc took their first dance as husband and wife, followed by Zulu and Gabi.

As the couples were eating cake, Zulu's phone rang. Looking at the caller ID, he groaned, seeing his sister's number come up. Gabi saw the image and smiled up at him.

"Take it, Quin," she said, kissing his cheek. "Maybe she wants to apologize." He loved her optimism, but he knew his sister was not calling to apologize.

"Hello."

Quincy.

"Hi, sis," he said casually.

Did you do it? Did you marry that woman?

"Yes, I did. I married the woman I love. The woman I plan on having children with and spending the rest of my life with, Quill. I wish you could just be happy for me."

Well, I guess you really did choose her over family. That's fine, Quincy. I was really hoping you would have come to your senses. You always did choose the rebel route.

"Rebel route? This is my life, Quill, not some racetrack. I chose the military because I wanted to serve, and if you'd been paying attention, I was a fucking Navy SEAL and a damned fine one! I chose to continue to serve through the Steel Patriots because I wanted to make a difference... with my brothers. I chose to marry Gabrielle because she is the most amazing woman on the planet and the only woman to make my heart beat. Because I can tell you it was damned sure dead before her."

You'll understand why I won't be visiting you, Quincy.

Her tone was harsh, filled with disgust and disdain, and it broke Quincy's heart that his sister felt so strongly about an error her husband made that she would blame a whole race of people. He knew racism existed on both sides, but he'd lived his life not caring about ethnicity, only serving.

"And I'm sure you'll understand when you won't be invited, Quill." He hung up the phone, sliding it into his back pocket. He turned to see the room of people he considered his family and the woman who was now the only thing that mattered in his life. Gabrielle brought light to a world that was half-dark to him; she brought love where there had been none before, and she brought hope to his hopeless soul.

"Everything okay?" she smiled up at him.

"Everything is perfect, baby."

CHAPTER TWENTY-FOUR

On Monday morning, Ace and Doc boarded an early flight to Sacramento. Ghost secured first-class seats for the two men, knowing that the extra room would be helpful for Ace. Doc watched the younger man, ensuring that at all times, his breathing and behavior were okay. Two hours into the flight, he finally turned to speak to him.

"You okay, brother?" he asked quietly so the other passengers couldn't hear.

"I am," he said with a small grin. "I hate that I'm this way, Doc. I don't want to be this way. You know that. I wish I could change it, wish it would just magically go away. I'm trying, really, I am."

"I know, brother, and I know that the meds recommended for you make you feel like shit, and I have mad respect that you're trying to do this on your own. Just remember, you're not really on your own. We all understand, Ace. We're all here for you, anything you need, and we'll be there for you." He nodded at his friend. Ace never really shared everything with him, but he was certainly willing to listen.

"You know, in the Navy, the other guys I worked with thought I was some sort of freak because of my IQ. They didn't have a clue why I was the way I was. I did fine with the physical stuff in boot camp until they wanted team events. You know the shit where we had to touch each other, work in close quarters. They just thought I was weird, and in the end, it was just easier to let them think that than to tell them the truth. I mean, it's not exactly a story people want to hear. I struggled so much those first few years, and of course, the Navy argued whether or not I was fit to serve."

"I can see them doing that," said Doc. "What made them allow you to stay?"

"My IQ mostly. The systems I was able to develop for naval intelligence. I was too valuable to them, so they started to accommodate my needs. I was given a wide berth, so to speak."

"You were pretty secretive with us, and we were working together every day. None of us knew you had any issues with closeness. It wouldn't have mattered to us, none of it. We respected your talent, and your skills kept us alive on more than one occasion." Ace nodded and looked out the window of the plane.

"Yea, I didn't want you guys to know what was wrong with me. I mean, I spoke to Ghost because I thought it was only fair he knew what was happening. He knew a lot of it, not all, but enough to know I wouldn't jeopardize your safety on a mission."

"What made you leave?" asked Doc.

"Lots of things. You guys were screwed over on the rescue of those girls. I knew the intel wasn't getting to you as it should. That little asshole from army intelligence was a piece of shit. He thought he was smarter than everyone else. I'd been pulled as your support the week before to work with the joint chiefs on something. I couldn't help myself, though. I kept following up on what he was sending to you guys and knew it wasn't the whole story. Pissed me off." Doc nodded.

"Yea, we knew something wasn't right. Definitely missed you on that little mission," he said with a smirk.

"Yea, well, I got back from that and found out what happened to you guys. Next thing I knew, they were shipping me to the forward operating base. I was forced to be in close quarters with five other guys, drunk, loud, smelly guys. I went to the base commander and explained the situation, told him to contact my former CO, but he was having none of it."

"Fuck, brother, I'm sorry." Ace nodded again and looked down. There was a boyish innocence and charm to his features, but he was all man.

"When... when my foster parents locked me in that cage, I was a child, not quite six yet. I had no idea that other children didn't live that way. They would play their music or television so loud it was horrible for me, like some sort of perverse desensitization training. I didn't know they were doing it so that if I screamed no one would hear me."

"Jesus, Ace," he whispered.

"Yea, I didn't really know Jesus at that point either. Their friends were all alcoholics or addicts as well. I guess I should be grateful that they didn't try to sexually assault me. I mean, most of the time, I didn't have any clothes on, but they didn't touch me sexually. It was more like taunting a wounded animal." He stared out at the blue sky, nothing to obstruct his thoughts except clouds.

"How did you get out?" asked Doc.

"One night, one of the couples they thought would be entertained... weren't. They left and contacted the authorities immediately. The police broke down the front door before the foster parents could move me. This big cop scooped me up in a blanket and sat me in the backseat of his cruiser. He didn't let me out of his sight.

"CPS was trying to find another foster family for me. One that dealt with victims of trauma, but that cop, he wouldn't let them take me. Officer John Mills was the most amazing man I'd ever met. I wasn't big enough to even go to school, severely underweight, malnourished, low on the height spectrum. I could barely read, but he didn't give a shit. He was divorced and fought for me from moment one. Homeschooled me for the first year, made sure I was in therapy three times a week, fed me, clothed me. He was so fucking patient, Doc. He was huge, six-three, big beefy hands. Considering where I came from, I should have been scared, but he was so kind, so gentle with me. I would wake from nightmares, and he would find me huddled in the closet. He would just open the doors, pull a blanket and pillow up next to me, and lay there all night with me. Sometimes talking to me, sometimes just lying there."

"I can only imagine what you were going through. He sounds like a great man who had a lot of love to give," said Doc.

"He was. All he ever wanted was for me to have a normal life, a healthy, normal life. He died about six years ago just as I was coming here. He was older when he took me in, but that didn't matter. He'd been in the Navy and then joined the force after he got out. I wanted to be just like him, but I knew being a cop wouldn't work for me at the time." Ace looked back at Doc and grinned.

"He saw me succeed, though, saw that I was able to make it work in the Navy and was so proud of me. I need to do this, get better for him. He gave me so much, Doc, so damned much. He dedicated his life to me, and I'll never forget that."

"Well, if it's any consolation, brother, you're doing fucking fantastic. Anything you need from me, ever, and I'll be there for you, Ace."

By the time they landed and gathered their luggage, it was early afternoon. Making their way to the home of the Dietrich family, Doc agreed to do most of the talking so that Ace could hang back.

The Dietrich's lived in a typical middle-class neighborhood in a small ranch-style home. There were two children's bikes in the front yard and an older model pickup truck parked in the driveway. Doc and Ace stepped up onto the porch and knocked. Opening the door was a man in his mid-thirties with black hair and brown eyes, a toddler attached to his hip.

"Can I help you?" he asked suspiciously.

"Mr. Dietrich? I'm Jack Harris, and this is my colleague Alex Mills. We're investigating an issue that may have ties to your wife's disappearance." The man eyed the two for a moment and then opened the screen door.

"Come in. Excuse the mess. I've got three kids, all under the age of nine, who have no concept of picking up after themselves. I work a full-time job, so I'm not exactly the neat housekeeper most people think I should be."

"No judgment here," said Doc, laughing with his hands in the air. Ace stayed behind him, stepping over toys and dirty clothes to find his way to a seat.

"You're here about my wife?" he asked, swallowing. "I'm not sure I understand. Are you with the police?"

"No, sir," said Ace, surprising Doc. "We're with an organization that looks into the disappearance of people, suspicious disappearances." Doc didn't feel the need to tell him everything about the Steel Patriots. It was a long fucking story. The man searched his face for something but just shook his head.

"Listen, my wife was a good woman at one time. We-we had our struggles like any young family. When Amy, the baby, was born, she-she just seemed more depressed than she had been with the first two. I was really worried about her, watched her closely. I came home from work early one day, hoping to surprise her."

"What happened?" asked Doc.

"She surprised me," he said sarcastically. "I walked in to hear my daughter screaming her lungs out in her crib. The two boys were napping, not sure how the fuck they were asleep, but they were. My wife was at the kitchen table with a needle full of heroin in her arm."

"I'm so sorry," said Ace.

"Yea, me too. I told her I couldn't have that with the kids in the house. She said she couldn't not have it... the drugs. Just that simple. She packed her shit and left, no arguments, no pleading. I would see her about once a week. She seemed to be able to clean herself up enough to swing by and see the kids, although in recent months, they didn't even care to see her anymore. Then she just stopped."

"Just like that?" asked Doc.

"Yea, I searched all the places she usually crashed, some really shitty, seedy places but didn't find her anywhere. Then one of the guys at this house she would sometimes crash said a guy approached her about a month ago and told her she could earn a ton of money."

"And what did she have to do to make this money?" asked Ace.

"It's not what you think or not what I thought anyway. I thought she was hooking on the side. Maybe she was, but this guy said the dude offered them all five grand for a simple surgery paid in full by the company he worked for. Said all they had to do was agree to give them a piece of their liver, a kidney, or a lung. I thought it was bullshit. I mean, all these people were addicts. Who in hell would want their organs?"

"That's what we're trying to figure out," said Doc.

"Well, that's when I went to the police. Weeks without any information, and then three days ago, they said they found an empty trailer in a junkyard filled with dead bodies. All of them were missing their internal organs."

"And your wife, she was amongst them?" asked Ace.

"Yea," he swallowed, looking down at the now sleeping face of his daughter. "She... Amy won't ever know her... won't know her mother."

"I'm so sorry," said Doc. "Where are your sons?"

"My folks took them for the day. It's been rough around here, and they just don't understand what's going on. The cops don't seem to give a shit about any of it since they were all drug addicts, hookers, homeless. Hell, I guess a part of me understands, but someone murdered my wife. She would have probably died by her own hand sooner or later but still."

"Did she leave you any money, cash?" asked Ace.

"Yea. How did you know that? I mean, I didn't even tell the cops for fear they would take it from me. The guys at the house said they were offering five grand, but she left an envelope under the front mat with ten grand in it. The cops said she was missing all her organs, so maybe that's why."

"I'm really sorry, sir," said Doc. He shrugged, looking back down at his sleeping child.

"I need to get her to bed. Is there anything else?"

"No, no, that's all," said Doc. "This is my card. If you hear anything else, think of anything else, please give us a call."

Doc and Ace quietly made their way to the airport hotel where they would be staying, neither saying a word. Tomorrow they would question the police and visit the junkyard where the bodies were found. Tonight, they both just wanted a shower and sleep.

CHAPTER TWENTY-FIVE

While Doc and Ace headed to the airport, Zulu rolled over to find Gabi sprawled on her stomach, her face away from his own, sound asleep. Her blanket of white hair was spread out behind her on her naked back, her skin marred by small red marks from his big rough fingers during their wedding night adventures. She was always willing and adventurous in bed, but last night was like his own fantasy porn film come to life.

When Gabi excused herself to get ready, he'd thought she might come out in a demure white negligee. He could not have been more wrong. Instead of virginal and white, she stepped from the bathroom in a pair of leather chaps, sky-high fuck-me boots, a leather bustier, and a silk black thong. The bustier barely contained her milky tits, and the rose-colored areolas were happily giving him a little peak.

"Son of a bitch," whispered Zulu.

"Do you like it?" she asked seductively, batting those big beautiful eyes.

"Like it? You're never taking that off," he grinned. His cock was standing straight up, and he couldn't help but reach down and stroke it, watching her move around the room.

"The girls said I would need leathers to ride with you when the weather got nicer. I bought a jacket too," she said, fanning herself despite the thirty-degree temperatures outside and the hundred-degree temperatures in the bedroom. "I just thought maybe I could practice riding you, in this," she said, waving a hand up and down.

"Come here," he growled. She smiled a slow, lazy smile at him and moved toward the bed. "Angel eyes, I said come here." She crawled up the bed, the creak of the leather almost deafening in the silent room. Straddling his thighs, he gripped her ass cheeks, squeezing. Taking the thong between his fingers, he yanked hard, ripping it from her body.

"Quin, seriously? That's the fourth pair you've ripped off my body. Why do I even bother?" she asked.

"I don't know, baby girl. That's a good question. Why do you even bother? I mean, I think I've made myself pretty clear. I like that pussy bare and waiting for me." She moved her hips forward, the wet heat of her core rubbing against his hard dick.

"Yea? You like this bare?" she asked innocently, running her fingers down her belly. Zulu could only respond with another low growl. She could only shake her head. He had no clue how wet that sound made her. "Let's see if you like this too." At the top of the cups of the bustier were tiny snaps. She flicked a thumb over them to lower the flap, revealing her breasts and nipples for him to enjoy.

"Fucking hell, where did you find this?" he asked. "Never mind, I don't want to know. Just buy as much as you want. Hell, buy out the whole damn store." He sucked her nipples so hard she thought she would be rubbing lotion on them for days. His thick, wet tongue wrapped around each, driving her to the point of orgasm and then pulling back. He unzipped the bustier and tossed it to the floor. Looking at her lower body wrapped in black leather, the contrast to her own skin, much like their skin when touching, made him want to blow without even penetrating her.

"I need you inside me, Quin," she moaned against his lips. "I need that big... thick... hot... cock inside me."

"Hmmm, lift, baby," he said, gripping her hips. "I love the boots, Angel eyes. You can wear those all day, every day." She smiled down at him as she lowered herself onto his waiting cock.

"Mmmm, yea, yea, that's the spot... the boots... right. Not good for riding... motorcycles... but good for riding you," she said with a sigh as she seated herself atop him. Gabi couldn't get enough of him. Gripping his head, she kissed him, sucking on his lips, tasting him, biting, nibbling. She rocked against him until she screamed her orgasm, but he wasn't done.

Flipping Gabi over, he raised her ass in the air and guided his big cock inside her once again, playing with her forbidden hole, filling her with his fingers. The sounds she made were more than his body could take. It was as if she were recording a phone sex call. He gripped a handful of hair, pulling back on her head as he drove harder and harder, filling her with everything he had. When she reached between them, her slender fingers playing with her clit, while another slid in beside his big thick piece of meat, he lost it all inside her. His body crashing to the bed, gasping for breath.

When he finally looked over to see if she was asleep, she was already playing with her tits getting ready for him again. He begged for a few minutes to recuperate, but she wouldn't hear of it, wrapping her sweet lips around him and having him hard within a matter of seconds.

Yea, it was exactly the way he would have wanted his wedding night to go, down to the exact detail. The wedding morning after? Not so much because the last thing he wanted to do was wake up and head to Atlanta.

He ran his big hands down her back, brushing her hair aside until his palm was flat against her beautiful white ass cheek. He could feel himself starting to get hard but immediately changed his thoughts to the mission and day ahead. Leaning over her, he brushed a kiss along her jaw, and he felt her smile.

"You better be careful," she said, without opening her eyes, "my sexy, domineering husband is a big scary motorcycle riding SEAL. If he finds you here, you're gonna be in big trouble."

"Nobody will ever touch this ass again, baby girl. No one but me that is. Your big, sexy, domineering, scary motorcycle riding SEAL," he growled, pulling her to him. "Good morning, Mrs. Slater."

"That sounds so wonderful," she said, kissing him. "Good morning, Mr. Slater. Thank you."

"For what?" he said, looking at her confused.

"For making my dreams come true. For trusting what we knew was real despite having not spent any time together. It was a big risk for both of us."

"Angel eyes, there is no risk in marrying the only woman I've ever loved, none." He kissed her again, smiling. "I hate to do this, but we gotta get up and get moving. The boys will be having breakfast about now. Pack a few things, and we'll head to the club." She nodded as she moved toward the shower with a backwards, come hither look. He shook his head laughing but couldn't help himself, making love to her once again in the shower before they walked to the club.

Doc and Ace were already gone, but Bree, Grace, and Kat were eating while the other guys talked about the plan for Atlanta.

"There they are!" yelled Eagle. "Have a good night, Angel eyes?" His devilishly handsome face smiled at her, and she knew he was trying to tease Zulu.

"We have a long drive ahead of us, Eagle," she said, smiling at him. "Do you really want to antagonize my husband in that way?" Zulu could only smile at the term husband.

"Listen up," said Ghost. "Cut your shit! This is fucking serious. You need to make sure Angel eyes is safe the entire time. If Zulu can't be by her side, you two will be. At no time is she to be left alone. Gunner? Zulu? Mathers has arranged for you two to meet with the local fed he's working with. Drop the twins and Gabi off at her apartment to get that shit done. Figure out what the fed knows, and then the five of you check into a hotel."

"I wanted to try and get to the hospital today, Ghost," she said quietly.

"I know you do, Gabi, but let's see what this fed knows first. We want to make sure you're not in any immediate danger. Once you make an appearance at the hospital, Dr. shithead will know you're alive." She nodded, noting that when he was serious, he used her real name, not Angel eyes.

"Alright, let's roll," said Gunner. "Eagle? Shotgun with me driving. Angel, you'll be flanked by Hawk and Zulu. Rules, honey, you go nowhere without one of us; you do as you're told, always, and," he handed her a small pistol, and she held it in her hand.

"I..."

"I know you probably don't know how to shoot, but just keep it in your purse. We'll give you some lessons along the way."

"Actually, I was going to say I'm better with a knife than a gun. Obviously, better with a knife," she said, grinning. "I took some self-defense classes, including weapons training. I'm a woman who lives alone—"

"Lived. You lived alone, baby. No more," said Zulu, hugging her to his side.

"Right," she smiled, "lived alone and worked in an inner-city emergency room. I've always been able to defend myself somewhat, although I have to say I froze with Gary and his hired hand." Gunner took the gun from her hand and placed a long, sheathed buck knife in it instead.

"That's more like it," she grinned.

Piling into the SUV, they left the compound headed south. On their third bathroom stop just outside of Atlanta, Zulu and Hawk saw the trouble coming.

Four rednecks stepped out of their pickup truck at the rest stop and stared at Gabi as if she were their next meal. Seeing the three white men step from the SUV and then Zulu, he knew what they were already thinking. So did Gabi.

"Just going to use the restroom, and I'll be right back," she said, kissing his lips. Hawk followed her, waiting outside the ladies' room. Gunner waited, watching the four men stand by their truck as if knowing what would happen. He saw Hawk holding Gabi's elbow as he escorted her back to the SUV and prayed they might leave without an incident.

Just as she was about to get into the vehicle, redneck number one stepped forward.

"Hey, blondie, whatchoo doin' with dem boys?" Gabi looked up at Zulu and winked at him. He wanted to rip their heads off, but something about that wink made him wait.

"Oh, you mean these boys?" she said, flinging a thumb over her shoulder. "Well, you see, I'm one of the sister wives, only opposite. They're my brother husbands. Yep, that's right. I'm a lucky girl. Four big strapping men, two are identical, and this one, I mean, damn, look at the size of his hands and feet if you know what I mean. We're headed to Atlanta for me to interview a few more. Just gotta have two things, boys, a big dick and a willingness to have fun with the boys here."

The four men were standing open-mouthed, staring at the blonde woman. Their eyes traveled from one man to the next, landing on the big black one hugging her close.

"You-You all touch each other?" asked one of them.

"Hey, don't knock it til you try it," said Eagle. "Kinda fun if you're secure in your manhood and all, and the lady loves watching, so it's a win-win for all of us."

"That's sick! Let's go, boys," he yelled to his buddies. Gabi gave them a disappointed pout and shrug and loaded into the vehicle. As they watched the pickup pull away, Gunner turned and grinned at her.

"Really? Brother husbands? That's what you came up with?"

"Hey, it was either that or a stable of studs for lonely housewives. They looked like they would buy into that one." Zulu shook his head, laughing as they continued down the highway.

Gabi directed Gunner to her apartment, where Hawk and Eagle were left with her while he and Zulu headed to the federal building downtown. She opened the door and immediately smelled the hint of copper, blood still soaked into her carpet and sofa.

Hawk looked at his brother with a raised eyebrow, and Eagle nodded. He searched the bedroom and closets to see if anything appeared disturbed, but honestly, he couldn't tell. Gabrielle had left in such a hurry it was difficult to tell if anything was out of place.

"Not much of a place, Angel eyes," said Eagle, looking around the tiny apartment. He expected something a little more hipster-vibe for Gabi.

"No, I know. I was pretty loaded down with student loans and debt. I was just getting it paid off when all this happened. My plan was to maybe buy myself a new car, maybe a little condo or townhouse. Now, well, I still need a decent car," she smiled, "but I guess I found my place to live."

"You can be sure you did, Angel," said Hawk. "And as for a car, why don't you let the boys in the shop work on your old car. It's not so bad, and there might be some things we can do to prolong the life of it. What do you want to take with you?"

"I guess all I really want is my clothes and books. I have a few things that belonged to my parents, photos, some dishes. I probably won't need more than a dozen boxes in all." Hawk nodded and started taping the boxes together. Three hours later, the last of the boxes was stacked, labeled, and ready for pick up. She looked at the boxes and sighed. Thirty-eight years of life held in a dozen boxes. That seemed pathetic at best.

Gabi heard the sharp knock on the door and thought it would be the delivery pickup or Zulu. Racing to the door, Eagle gripped her around the waist, lifted her, and pulled her back, shaking his head.

"We answer the door, Angel eyes, not you." She nodded, standing behind him as Hawk opened the door.

"Can I help you?" he asked sharply, staring at the man in front of him. Dr. Gary Scott just stared up at the big man and then behind him to the identical twin, and still further back, the woman he was looking for.

"I'd like to speak to Dr. London. Alone," he said with an air of superiority. Eagle looked behind him.

"Let me guess. That's Dr. shithead," he said, looking back at Gabrielle. Gabi giggled and nodded.

"Not fucking happening, asshole," said Hawk. "In fact, I understand you like to hurt women, so why don't I let you know how that feels? Maybe break a few fingers or a wrist. That would be good, wouldn't it?" Hawk took a step forward, forcing Gary Scott to step back from the door.

"Look, I-I don't want any trouble. It was all a misunderstanding. Gabrielle! Gabrielle, tell them we're friends, more than friends," he yelled.

"More than friends?" she shrieked. "Are you fucking kidding me? You turned me over to that animal, and he beat me half to death. If you think for one moment you and I were ever friends, you've lost your mind, and you know damned good and well we have NEVER, and I do mean NEVER, been anything beyond colleagues."

"I believe the lady has spoken," said Hawk, shoving a hand against the chest of Gary Scott.

"You'll regret this, Gabrielle! I'll ruin you. I'll make sure you never operate again! You'll be sorry that you turned me away!"

"You won't do a fucking thing," said the deep voice behind him. Gary Scott turned and looked up and up and up to stare into a very angry face. "You ever come near her again, breathe in her direction, so much as utter her name, and the earth will be relieved of your existence. You feel me, little man?"

"I-I just want to talk to her. It's professional. You wouldn't understand."

"We have nothing to talk about," said Gabi. "I'll be turning in my resignation, and I won't need your reference. I know what you're doing, Gary. I will stop you."

Gary Scott wanted to scream at her, wanted to tell her she would be dead by morning, but he knew he couldn't deliver on that promise, especially with her own personal protection detail. Instead, he turned and left the apartment, already making plans for moving on to the next hospital.

CHAPTER TWENTY-SIX

"You okay, baby?" asked Zulu, hugging her to his body.

"I'm great," she smiled as the last of the boxes were loaded on the delivery truck. "I'm all packed up and ready to start my new life with you." He nodded at her, pulling her close. He kissed the top of her head, inhaling the scent of her shampoo and perfume combined.

"Why don't you check one more time and make sure you didn't forget anything, Angel eyes? The boys and I will wait in the hallway, and then we'll turn in your key." She nodded, moving around the small space, opening and shutting cabinets and closets. Zulu turned to Hawk and Eagle.

"Did he touch her?" he said through a clenched jaw. His big fists were curled at his sides, and Hawk noticed the dangerous pulsing vein throbbing at his neck.

"Don't insult us, brother," said Hawk. "He didn't get close enough and wouldn't have as long as one of us was breathing. He was probably just trying to bully her. Wanted to get her alone, but we weren't going to let that happen."

"He'll be running scared now," said Gunner. "Might make him nervous, make him do something stupid, or he just might run, leave the hospital." Zulu nodded.

"Fed said they've had a few complaints of missing veterans, homeless, just like the other cities. They don't have anything to pin on Scott, but anything we can provide would sure help them. Problem is just his little push and shove act with Angel eyes ain't enough. She could file an assault charge on him, but it's her word against his. Even the fed said Scott would claim he didn't know the other man, and the garage footage has mysteriously disappeared from their security cameras." Eagle nodded, hearing the door open behind them. He smiled at Gabi and waved for her to follow.

"All good, baby?" asked Zulu.

"Yea, everything is good. That was just a place to lay my head, not a home. With you is where my home is. I'm happy, Quin, really happy," she said, hugging him.

"Me too, Angel."

A short drive later found them pulling into the hotel, a huge upscale boutique hotel in downtown Atlanta, the three-story lobby gleaming with marble floors and chandeliers hanging from the thirty-foot ceilings. As they checked in, Gunner pulled Hawk and Eagle to the side.

"I need for you two to try and find Max Kaler's children. The fed said they'd been looking for the daughter who filed the complaint but can't locate her. This is the address where the brother and sister lived." Both men nodded and left the lobby.

"Where are Hawk and Eagle going?" asked Gabi.

"They're headed out to have a little fun," said Gunner. "Why don't you two drop your bags, and let's meet for dinner?" Zulu nodded, knowing exactly where Eagle and Hawk were going. Entering their room, Gabi turned and smiled at Zulu.

"I guess we can make this a mini-honeymoon," she said, smiling. Zulu felt like shit. He'd totally forgotten that this was technically their honeymoon. He knew he wanted to take Gabi somewhere special, but it damned sure wasn't Atlanta.

"I'm sorry, Angel eyes, so fucking sorry for all this. I promise when we're done, you and me will go somewhere special, anywhere you want to go," he said, kissing her forehead.

"Quin? This is special, being here with you. This is all I've ever wanted. I don't need any fancy trips. When this is done, let's just lock ourselves in the house for a week."

"I love you so much, baby. I used to wake up from my dreams and think I was going fucking bat-shit crazy. I was so damned worried about my own mental health. You were all I could see, and every woman I met was being compared to what I thought was just a dream. Then you walked right through my doors and took my breath away."

"Oh, Quin," she said with a sniffle, "don't you know that's exactly how I feel. I was so scared when I rolled into that parking lot. I mean, it was New Year's Eve. I thought for sure you'd have a woman or God help me, two curled around your gorgeous body. I was worried you wouldn't remember me or even want me. Then when I saw your face looking down at me from the exam table, I-I just lost all my breath."

"Awe, babe, I love you so very much," he said, kissing her face. Just as he was about to do more than kiss, a loud knock on the door told them Gunner was hungry.

"I guess that's our cue," she smiled, "but later, later you're mine, Mr. Slater."

CHAPTER TWENTY-SEVEN

Doc and Ace drove toward the salvage yard where the bodies were discovered. It wasn't exactly in the best part of town, and neither had weapons with them, so they were more than a little cautious with their surroundings.

Sitting back off the road was a massive junk and salvage yard, the fences seemingly bulging at the seams with the mountains of scrap. Driving through the gates, they parked at a small trailer with a rusted sign indicating it was the office. Ace stepped out first, only to realize two large Doberman Pinschers were headed straight for him. He stilled, watching the dogs, and then raised a hand. Both dogs stopped abruptly. He lowered his hand in a quick motion, and they promptly sat in front of him.

"Who the fuck are you, and what have you done to my dogs?" growled a man from the trailer door, his hand firmly gripping a double-barreled shotgun.

"Haven't done anything except teach them some manners," said Ace kneeling to pet the dogs. "We're not here to hurt them or you. We just need to ask you some questions."

"You a cop?" Ace shook his head. "A fed?"

"You got a problem with law enforcement?" asked Doc with a grin.

"Nope, just don't like people pokin' in my business. Now, who are you, and what do you want?" he asked in a less than hospitable tone.

"My name is Alex Mills, and this is Jack Harris. We'd like to ask you some questions about the bodies found in the tractor-trailer on your property." The old man eyed them up and down and lowered the shotgun. He stepped down off the porch and walked toward them, snarling at the dogs in disappointment as he passed.

"It's at the back of the property. Follow me. Already told the cops it would be easy enough to get to it through the fence. Been tellin' 'em for months that kids cut a hole in my fence and been stealin' from me. Course they don't do nothin' bout it since I'm just a junkman and all. I can't afford to repair the fence, but the dogs usually keep everyone out." He glared back at the dogs as if to say, 'usually.'

"Did they bark abnormally in the last few weeks?" asked Doc.

"Naw, they pretty much bark at anything and everything, so I don't mind 'em too much." Ace rolled his eyes, wondering why in the hell he had the dogs if he didn't pay attention to them. The old man kept walking toward the back of the property as they picked their way past rusted-out cars, trailers, appliances, anything, and everything someone might be able to salvage.

"Did you know any of the victims?" asked Ace. The old man's head popped up, and he looked back at Ace with a fierce expression.

"Didn't know none of 'em! Told the cops that. That young woman, the Dietrich girl, she'd hang around here every now and then just lookin' for someplace safe to lay her head, but I didn't really know her. Never hurt nothin', just would find an old car seat and go to sleep. She'd be gone within a few hours. Broke my heart she didn't have no one to care about her."

"Did she ever talk to you?" asked Doc.

"Sometimes," he nodded. "She talked 'bout her kids and husband. Said she did 'em wrong but didn't know how to make it right. Felt damned sorry for her. She wasn't right, ya know, in the head. She was just lookin' for somethin' to make all the pain go away. Not a drug user myself, but know enough folks who did it because they wanted the pain to go away. That's all that gal wanted."

"Did she ever express concern for her own safety? Maybe someone following her or chasing her?" asked Ace.

"Nothin' like that. Said some man offered her a lot of money for somethin'. I told her to be careful. I mean, he coulda' been one of them whack jobs that steals women and ties 'em up or somethin'. She said it wasn't nothin' like that. He was gonna give her a ton of money for a kidney or somethin'. Told her it was all bullshit on account of her drug use. Told her no one wanted a kidney from no drug user."

"Did she give you the name of the man?"

"Nope, didn't ask," he said, stopping. "Try to stay outta folks' business. Keeps me alive longer. 'Cept that little girl didn't deserve what she got. That's the trailer. Noticed the smell, and the dogs were avoidin' the area for 'bout a week. I knew that smell, smelled it before. Called the cops, and you know the rest." Ace nodded at the man, the faint smell of death still emanating from the trailer.

"Cops said they'd come get the trailer as evidence but ain't nobody come to git it yet. You know where to find me," he said, walking back toward the trailer. "Be careful you don't cut yerselves."

Ace watched as the man disappeared, but the dogs stayed at his side. Doc looked down and grinned, shaking his head.

"How'd you do that?" he asked, looking at the dogs.

"Simple," he said, digging in his jacket pocket. He pulled out two long pieces of bacon and held them out to the dogs. "I just assumed a salvage yard would have a dog or two. Played well for me."

"Ace, you're something else!" barked Doc. He opened his backpack and pulled out two masks for him and Ace. "It won't block the smell completely, but maybe enough that we can get a look inside the trailer. Put some gloves on as well." Ace nodded, donning the mask and gloves.

As Doc opened the trailer doors, the wave of death hit them smack dab in the face. All the bodies were removed, but the smell of blood was so prevalent it clung to every crevice of the trailer. Doc climbed up first. Taking his flashlight, he scanned the floors looking for anything. The wooden slats were soaked a dark wine stain from the blood. Nothing was left untainted by the death that had been piled inside the trailer.

"Jesus," said Ace. "How many bodies were in here?"

"Five."

"Seems an awful lot of blood for five bodies," he said, looking at Doc. Doc looked at the other man and nodded. He was right. The bodies would have been dead when placed in the trailer, which meant most of the blood would have already been drained. Why was there so much blood in the trailer?

"You don't think they were put in here and weren't dead yet, do you?" asked Ace.

"Christ! I hope not," said Doc, shaking his head. "If that's true, we're dealing with some seriously sick fucks." He nodded toward the door indicating that he'd seen enough. He took a few quick photos and jumped from the back of the trailer, securing the doors once more.

"What now?" asked Ace.

"Now we go home and see what the others have found."

CHAPTER TWENTY-EIGHT

The hotel had three restaurants on various floors. The main dining room was on the first floor next to a long, sleek bar with the usual business patrons having their after-work cocktail along with hotel guests. Gunner, Zulu, and Gabi chose the restaurant attached to the bar so they would have a clear line of sight to the front doors when Hawk and Eagle returned.

"Evening, folks," said the smiling waiter. He looked like a typical twenty-something college student, his hair neatly tied in a topknot, his teeth too white to be natural. "What can I get you to drink besides water?"

"I'll have a glass of merlot," said Gabi, smiling at the young man. He looked down at her, just staring, not looking away, his gaze directed at her eyes and hair. He felt a hard nudge and looked at the offender.

"You wanna keep staring, junior, or should I maybe get your manager?" asked Gunner.

"S-sorry, really, I'm so sorry. It's just your eyes are amazing. I'm terribly sorry," he said, swallowing.

"I'll have a beer, anything on draft," said Gunner.

"Same," growled Zulu. He nodded, leaving the table.

"He didn't mean anything by it, guys. I'm used to it. I don't even really notice people staring anymore. I mean, not really." That was a lie, but she didn't want them to feel the need to jump to her defense any longer.

"Doesn't matter, Angel eyes," said Gunner. "Staring is rude no matter what, but when you're with us, there's no need to have to tolerate that shit."

"Well, thank you. I guess I'm just not used to anyone defending me." Gunner eyed Zulu and then looked back at Gabi.

"What do you mean, baby? You never had a man defend you?" asked Zulu.

"N-no, not really. I mean, my dad always tried to with the neighborhood kids, but eventually, he just thought I should defend myself, and I guess that was the right thing to do. In school, well, kids can be cruel, you know that. Teachers never stepped in, ever. In fact, some of the teachers were the worst offenders. I had one that was positive I was some sort of devil child or an abomination against Gods' children. She was a real piece of work. High school was the worst for me because the girls all thought I was a freak, or if they didn't, they saw me as a threat to their boyfriends, who were always staring at me. I didn't want any part of it. I didn't want any part of them. I just wanted to graduate and get the hell out. I was a serious student and just wanted to get into medical school.

"In college, I had a few dates here and there, but most of the time, it was guys trying to see if the freak was truly freaky," she blushed, looking down at her glass of wine. "After medical school, I had two serious boyfriends, but both cheated on me, and I dumped them. End of story."

"Damn right, it's the end of the story," said Zulu. "No need to ever relive that shit again, baby." She could only smile as the waiter returned to take their order. A few minutes later, Gabi looked at Gunner.

"So, tell me your story, Gunner. Girlfriend? Interested party?" she smiled.

"Oh, man," smiled Zulu, "here we go." Gunner stopped his hand, a bite of bread ready for the tasting.

"Beautiful, I'd do just about anything for you, but if you try to fix me up, we're done. I don't need a woman permanently in my life.

Occasionally, in my bed, but not in my life, and as cute as they are, I don't want any damned kids," he said, grinning. Gabi shook her head and smiled. "Not much to tell, gorgeous. Like I said before, I have two brothers, was in the marines for sixteen years, love to ride, shoot, drink, oh and eat. Had a girlfriend once, long time ago now." Even Zulu was surprised to hear that. He'd never heard Gunner discuss a woman before.

"Were you serious?" asked Gabi quietly.

"Yea, guess you could say that. We dated about two years, and I was gonna propose to her while on leave. Showed up at her door to find her about six months pregnant. I had been deployed for almost a year, so, yea, that ended well."

"Geez, I'm so sorry I brought it up, Gunner. I will never understand a woman that cheats on a man or a man cheating on a woman, but to do it while they're deployed is just despicable to me. I'm so very sorry about that."

"Not your fault, Angel eyes," he said, taking a bite of his pasta. "I was young – twenty-three – so it seems a lifetime ago. Besides, at the rate my brothers are falling, I'll have enough female influence around me to last my entire life." Zulu cut into his steak, and the conversation turned to football as Eagle and Hawk came through the door looking around the lobby. As if sensing they were being watched, they moved toward the table, sitting down.

The waiter immediately came over and took their order, rushing to get their food in so they could eat with the rest of their table.

"What did you find out?" asked Zulu.

"Brother was there, but the sister has been missing for three days. He said she had a date with a doctor." Hawk eyed the rest of the table, and they knew exactly who she went out with.

"Damn! You think she went out with Gary?" asked Gabi.

"Think so, beautiful," said Eagle. "Brother said she went to see their father at the hospital and went round and round with someone about him not being there. She told her brother a 'really nice doctor' tried to help her and then took her to dinner. She ended up spending a few intimate hours with him."

"That's all?" asked Gunner. Eagle shook his head.

"Nope. Brother said his sister got anxious about not being able to find their father. Haven't seen him in like seven years, but she knew where he usually stayed. He said she was hell-bent on finding him, and when she couldn't, she filed a missing persons' report telling them about her encounter at the hospital. Two nights later, she got a call from the doctor inviting her to dinner again."

"The brother said when she didn't return, he filed a report with the police," said Hawk, "but cops told him she was an adult, and they had to wait forty-eight hours. He says his sister never stays out all night. He also said the father left them an envelope with five grand inside, cash."

"Jesus," whispered Gabi. "Where is he getting the cash? I mean, he has to be withdrawing it from somewhere, or someone is giving it to him, right?" All eyes turned to her and grinned.

"He's not working alone," said Gunner, staring off in space. "He can't be."

"But who would benefit? I mean, if they're doing this to political rivals, corporate heads, that sort of thing, how do we narrow that down? It sounds like someone literally wanting to play God," said Gabi.

"Can't solve it tonight," said Gunner. "Let's get some sleep, and we'll all go with you to the hospital tomorrow, Angel. Rules still apply, Gabi. You go nowhere without us tomorrow. If you enter the doctors' lounge, we go with you; any records area, we go with you. Nothing happens without us beside you. Understand?" She nodded.

Gunner looked at the other men and, using their secret, silent language, said everything they all knew. Someone was playing God, and they were going to stop him come hell or high water.

CHAPTER TWENTY-NINE

Gabi was nervous stepping inside the hospitals' emergency room the next morning. It was relatively quiet for an inner-city emergency room. She noticed a patient with abdominal pain in one of the bays and then another with what appeared to be a sprained wrist, but nothing urgent. The eyes of the staff members followed her. Some gave her a slight nod, others a look of annoyance and dismissal as they watched her entourage. Gabi stopped at the desk and spoke softly to the woman behind the counter.

"Hi, Tammy," she said, smiling down at the woman.

"Dr. London! Oh my goodness, it's so nice to see you! Dr. Scott said you had a family emergency. Is everything okay?" she asked, seeming genuinely concerned.

"Yes, everything is fine. In fact, I'd like to introduce you to my husband, Quincy Slater, and his brothers." Gabrielle's face remained stoic, not a hint of teasing or jest as the other woman looked each man up and down. She could see out of the corner of her eye another woman approaching from her left and knew what was coming. None of the nurses were overly kind to her, but Carla was more in the bitch realm.

Sidling up to the desk, the ER nurse greeted Gabi coldly at first, then realizing the men were with her, she plastered a smile on her face, eyeing Hawk and Eagle up and down.

"Dr. London! I didn't realize that was you. It's so lovely to see you," she said, oozing sweetness and bullshit. "We've missed you so much! Who are these handsome gentlemen?"

Gabi wanted to smack the hell out of the woman. She was never friendly to her and definitely never treated her with respect. She was looking at the twins like they were an all-you-can-eat buffet as she flipped her long brown ponytail over her shoulder and batted her big brown eyes at the men, the huge fake tits pressed against the counter.

"No one you need to know," said Gabi confidently, ignoring the woman. "Is Dr. Scott here?" The woman's mouth opened and closed, her hand on her hip in a show of defiance.

"I believe my *wife* asked you a question," said Zulu, casting his big shadow over the smaller woman. He wasn't in the habit of intimidating women, but this one he knew caused pain to Gabi in her past, and he wouldn't tolerate that for a minute.

"Y-your... your w-wife?"

"That's right. Choose your words wisely. Where is Dr. Scott?" he asked.

"I don't know. He called out today. I thought maybe you were here to cover for him," she said, looking down at the chart.

"Well, I'm not," said Gabi, staring her down. "I need to gather my things, and then I'll drop by human resources to give my notice."

"You're leaving us, Dr. London?" asked Tammy, looking somewhat forlorn.

"I'm afraid so. My place is with my husband." The nurse looked from Gabi to the other men, lingering a little too long on the twins once again.

"And just where is that place?" she asked in a haughty tone.

"None of your fucking business," said Gunner quietly, leaning forward. She stepped back and swallowed, but as the group walked past her, she gripped Eagle's arm and leaned in.

"If you and your twin want someone to show you around, just give me a call any time. Name is Carla," she said, winking at him. Eagle looked down at her hand holding his arm, and pulled away.

"Sorry, I prefer my women to have souls." She gasped as if slapped in the face. "Oh, and disease-free." He followed the long line of his teammates and Gabi toward the staff locker room. She gathered her few items into her bag and then pointed to Dr. Scott's locker.

It took only a matter of seconds for Hawk to break into the locker, noting it was completely empty. He'd most likely cleared his things out the day before and was long gone.

"Now what, baby?" asked Zulu.

"We need to see if there are any John or Jane Does in the morgue," she said, looking at the men. The twins groaned and rolled their eyes but followed her to the elevator bank. When they reached the morgue, she spoke casually to the attendant, who confirmed that there were no unnamed patients but that there had been several just a few days ago. He assumed the funeral home had taken them.

"What was the name of the funeral home that picked up the John Does?" asked Gabi.

"Pearsons. Always Pearsons picking up the Does," he said, turning to get back to the stacks of work facing him. Gabi just nodded, turning to join the others.

Gabi then headed back upstairs to pull the records of the patients who'd been admitted but showed no release dates and crossed reference that with surgeries that were unscheduled. She leaned back in the chair, staring at the computer.

"It's gone," she whispered. "It's all gone. The records I saw before. The admits. They're all gone. He wiped the system."

"Damn!" growled Gunner.

"Nothing more to do here," said Zulu. "Let's head home."

"What about the funeral home?" asked Gabi. "They might know something. Should we check it out or have Ace check it out?" Gunner nodded but said nothing else.

"We'll figure it out, honey," said Zulu.

They all nodded as they walked out of the hospital. Gabi felt a deep warmth come over her. She was leaving the place she'd lived for the last five years behind. The place that she never called her own, never felt comfortable in. Instead, she was going with the man of her dreams to start her new life. Home.

CHAPTER THIRTY

"I'm almost there now," he said to the caller. "Yes, I know. I know. I said I fucking know! You don't have to tell me what kind of danger we're in or how we'll all go to jail if we're found out. I know." He hit the silent button on the phone and looked at the man seated beside him.

"Here are your new papers," he said, handing the other man the envelope. "You'll now be Dr. Scott Edwards. Your credentials are updated, your licensing, everything. The hospital is expecting you tomorrow."

He nodded at the other man. Gary Scott. Scott Edwards. What did it matter anymore? He was born David Fishbein to immigrant parents, but over the years, he'd been Dr. David Walters, Dr. Walter Hayes, Dr. Hayes Carter, and so many more he couldn't remember. In fact, there were days he couldn't remember much of anything except how to harvest an organ.

It all seemed so easy at first. A simple way to make extra money and pay off his student loans. Then it snowballed. One kidney wasn't enough. One lung turned into three. Then it was a constant demand.

Even when he started to refuse, he was pressured and blackmailed for more.

He was now at his tenth hospital in as many years and knew his time was running out. Yes, he was the brains behind the surgeries, but there were so many moving parts he didn't see and didn't want to see. He wasn't sure he would ever be free of these people.

"Losing your nerve, Dr. Edwards?" asked Karl.

"No," he said, snatching the envelope with his new papers. "Just thinking that I need a nice long vacation when this is done."

"When this is done? It will never be done. Don't you get it? This? This arrangement will never be done. Believe me, our employers will make sure we have enough work to last a lifetime."

That's exactly what he was afraid of. More work than he could handle. He hadn't thought much of having a family or settling down until the little hottie in Atlanta. Of course, he had to permanently shut her mouth, but if not, she would have been a good solid choice for a wife. She had great hips, perfect for babies; she was freaky as hell in the bedroom, and she gave a blow job like a professional.

"Are you still there?" asked the voice on the car speaker.

"Yes, we're still here," said Karl, taking the phone off mute. "I was just giving him his papers."

"Fine. You have your orders. I need a liver and two lungs by next Monday. They've already been ordered and paid for. Have Karl contact transport when they're ready, and we'll get them to the buyers."

"Understood, but do you understand that this cannot continue forever? Sooner or later, someone is going to catch up with us, and it will be the end of this little money-making adventure."

"Don't tell me what I can and cannot do, doctor. And you're dumber than I thought if you think this is about making money. If I wanted money, I'd sell drugs or guns. Hell, selling humans would make more money than this. This is about power, and right now, I'm the one with all the power. Remember that, doctor."

The call disconnected, and he looked down at the stacks of papers in his lap. A new passport, new diploma and transcripts, recommendations from other hospitals, everything someone with a new identity would need. The question was, how in the hell did they get all this and ensure that when the references were checked, it all came back okay.

"Let's go, doc," said Karl. "I'll drop you at your new townhouse and then get settled in my place. I'll let you know when I find our first package. You just be ready."

He nodded at the man, watching the winter sky flash by the car window.

"Did you hear me, doc? You need to be ready."

"I heard you. I'll be ready." Don't worry about me, he thought. I'll be ready. I'll be more than ready when the time comes.

CHAPTER THIRTY-ONE

It was late afternoon by the time the team returned to Club Steel. What should have been nine hours was a measly seven with Gunner at the wheel.

Doc and Ace were already seated with Ghost and Whiskey, filling them in on what they'd found in Sacramento. When the others walked in, Ghost nodded at them to put their things away and return when they were rested.

Gabi and Zulu placed their bags inside the house, grabbed a quick shower, and then returned to the restaurant knowing the others would want to discuss their findings as quickly as possible. George pulled Gabi into a big hug, kissing her forehead with a smile. A few moments later, he set plates in front of each of them, filled with their supper.

"How was it?" asked Ghost. Gabi shrugged.

"As expected. I wasn't exactly the popular doctor at the hospital. I cleaned out my locker and gave my notice, but when we went into Gary's locker, it was completely empty, not even a receipt for a cup of coffee. I think he got nervous when he saw that I wasn't alone and ran."

"Why would he do that?" asked Whiskey.

"He came to the apartment when I was boxing up my stuff," she said quietly.

"Say what?" yelled Whiskey. Kat patted his arm and winked at Gabi.

"Settle down, baby," said Kat softly. "Let her speak, and then you'll have your answers. Remember your big words."

"Thanks, Kat. Eagle and Hawk were helping me box up my things when he knocked on the door. Demanded that the two of them leave us alone so he could talk to me. Let's just say that didn't go too well. Zulu and Gunner arrived and scared the shit out of him. He left, and that's the last we saw of him."

"What about the daughter of Max Kaler? What did she have to say?" asked Ghost.

"Nothing. Can't find her. Her brother filed a missing persons' report on her," said Gunner. "She went on a date, twice from what we can gather, with Gary Scott, and this second time she didn't return."

"Shit! What the fucking hell is going on here?" Ghost dragged his fingers through his hair, sighing as he did.

"I'm honestly not sure myself," said Gabi. "Organ transplanting is highly complicated and complex. Teams have to work within a time frame so exact, so precise, no one can screw up, or the patient is dead, and the organ is useless. It's why I suspected that all of this was not on the up-and-up. There's too much at risk here, especially arbitrarily taking organs from random people. Even if they're doing it for nefarious reasons, they still have to keep the organ viable."

"Think of what they would need at their disposal. An operating room, transportation to get the organ to where it's needed, surgeons, nurses, anesthetists. There is no other conclusion. They are doing this to harm others intentionally. My question is around the support team," she finished.

"What do you mean, support team?" asked Kat.

"Well, to get the organ is one thing, and we know that Gary appears to be doing that. But someone on the other end is putting it into the patient without question. They're not asking where it was harvested from, the blood type, patient history, nothing. There has to be an entire team of people working together to pull this off. Who has that kind of power and connection?" Ghost nodded at the doctor for her very astute summary of the situation.

For several weeks now, he'd been thinking exactly the same thing. This was a network of people working together on this, and to what purpose? Knock out a political or corporate rival? There were easier ways of getting rid of someone, and a bullet, sure as shit, was cheaper.

Ace stepped toward the table and pulled out a chair so that he was sitting slightly away from the others yet still within the circle.

"Heard you did a stellar job in Sacramento, brother," said Gunner. Ace nodded, a small grin on his lips.

"Thanks, but Doc is pretty easy to travel with. I have some news," he said calmly. "First is that Max Kaler's daughter was pulled from the Chattahoochee River this morning. She was unidentifiable at first, but they got prints and confirmed an hour ago with an ID from her brother. Simple knife to the heart. No organs missing, but she was beaten, and although they don't think she was raped, there was evidence of a sexual encounter prior to death."

"He wouldn't take her organs," said Gabi, "all fingers would point right back at him if he removed her organs and left her to die. Plus, if he's doing what we think, her organs are healthy. He wouldn't need them."

"Dr. Gary Scott gave his notice at South Atlanta General this morning as well, just shortly after you left the hospital, via e-mail. Just on a hunch, I decided to do a little digging." Ghost grinned at the other man and nodded.

"And pray tell, what did you find?"

"Dr. Gary Scott doesn't exist." Ace said it as if he were reciting the ingredients to a recipe. No nonsense, just facts.

"Wh-what? Of course, he does. I worked with him."

"I don't mean like that. He physically exists, but that name does not exist as a surgeon. Fortunately, Gary Scott travelled to Canada for a conference last year, which meant his fingerprints were in a database accessible to, well, to me. Gary Scott is actually David Fishbein. Forty-four years old, graduate of Cornell and the University of Pennsylvania. Eleven years ago, he was drowning in debt, like more than three hundred thousand to college loans, credit cards, two mortgages. You name it, and he owed them."

"Jesus," whispered Gabi. "I mean, I had student loans and debt, but three hundred grand?"

"Yea, seems he received loans from a questionable source. He also had a bit of a problem betting on the games. Owed more than five hundred thousand to a loan shark in Vegas. Suddenly, two months later, his debts are all paid. Every penny. No checks deposited or cashed, nothing."

"Wait? He got almost a million in cash from someone?" asked Kat.

"Not exactly. He received a direct deposit from a company called ERG Industries. I've tried to track down their location, but nothing. On paper, they don't exist."

"Then what do we do?" asked Gabi.

"I said they don't exist on paper, Angel," smiled Ace. "Everyone exists in cyberspace. You just have to give me some time to find them. For now, you all let me do what I do best, and you do what you do best." Ace stood and headed back to his computer room without another word.

"Gary isn't Gary," said Gabi with disbelief. "Wow, I mean, I knew there was something off about him, but honestly, I just thought it was him being a sleazeball." Everyone nodded as they returned to their meal. A few minutes later, Ghost picked up his cell phone, chatting quietly away from the table. When he finished, he looked at the group.

"Seems we're raising eyebrows in D.C.," he said, looking at everyone. "Gabrielle? You, Gunner, Zulu, and the twins are meeting Senators Kantek and Jette at Old Ebbitt Grill tomorrow at one. They both serve on the ethics commission and want to know what you know. Mathers will meet you there."

"Damn, Angel eyes," said Hawk. "Your first month here, and you're already being summoned to Washington. Way to go!" He high-fived Gabi, but she wasn't sure it was something worth high-fiving over. Her expression was one of fear and concern but also uncertainty.

"What's up, Angel eyes?" asked Gunner.

"I... I don't know. Something about this doesn't feel right. I mean, beyond the obvious. Why would a couple of senators want to meet with me?"

"Well, if there's one thing we all know," said Doc, "is that if it doesn't feel right, it probably isn't. Trust your gut." She nodded.

"Okay. Then tomorrow, if I don't say everything, tell everything, just know that it's intentional." Zulu looked at his wife with worry, then pulled her in for a kiss.

"No one I trust more than you, baby girl, except my brothers." Gabi excused herself for a moment, headed to Ace's workspace. A few moments later, she returned feeling slightly relieved.

"What's up, baby?" asked Zulu.

"Nothing right now, just wanted to make sure I gave Ace some thoughts about the files we were reviewing." He nodded, knowing that she didn't tell him everything. He'd let her have this moment, but they would have a discussion about disclosing everything to each other.

For now, he was just happy having her in his arms one more night.

CHAPTER THIRTY-TWO

Gabi pulled on the warm flannel pajama bottoms and a matching camisole, then grabbed Quincy's sweatshirt and pulled that on as well. She lifted a sleeve and inhaled, taking in the masculine scent of her husband. Her hair was pulled up high in a ponytail, and she wiped all her makeup off her face and then shuffled to the living room where Zulu was stoking the fire.

"Hey, beautiful," he said, pulling her into his side. He kissed her lips as she wound her arms around his neck, deepening the kiss. Her delicate fingers massaged the back of his head as her body molded against his own.

"Wow! What did I do to deserve that?" he asked breathless.

"You loved me," she smiled. Zulu lifted her in his arms and then set them both on the sofa, facing the heat of the fireplace.

"Angel eyes, you never owe me anything for loving you, something that comes as natural as breathing. Nothing will change my mind about that, nothing, baby." Gabi curled into his big body tighter, her knees up near her own chest. The crackle of the fire was the perfect backdrop as they listened to the wind whistling outside and the snow flying by the windows.

"Looks like more snow tonight," she said quietly.

"Yea, we might have to postpone D.C. tomorrow. We'll take a look at the weather in the morning and decide."

"Well, now," she said, smiling, "wouldn't that be a shame? I mean, locked up here with you for a few days, snowed in. Terrible, just terrible." Zulu laughed, pulling her onto his lap. It was as if he couldn't get close enough. Lying her back against the sofa, he lay his big body along hers, supporting his weight on his elbows.

Gabi could feel his rock-hard length against her stomach and the immediate pooling of warmth and wetness between her legs. The feel of his muscles against her softness added to her already heightened senses as she involuntarily moaned against his lips.

Zulu gripped Gabi tightly to his body and twisted in one swift motion, letting her lay on top of his big body. Her hair fell forward onto his chest, a tiny laugh escaping those lush lips, her eyes sparkling at him in the firelight. It was the dawning of a sudden memory.

"I remember everything," he whispered, staring into her face. She pulled back, staring down at him with a small smile. "Before... before I remembered your face, I remembered the kiss, but now, having you above me like this."

"What do you remember?" she said, kissing him sweetly.

"Your voice. You talked to me the entire time, and when I didn't hear your voice, I was panicked. I remember hearing the wind like tonight, except there was thunder and lightning. You told me you were scared, and all I could think about was trying to keep you safe, but I wasn't even awake." She nodded, smiling down at him. "You crawled in the bed next to me. You just lay your hand on my chest, and I thought it was the most beautiful thing I'd ever experienced. You didn't touch me inappropriately at all. You just held my hand and lay your other hand on my chest."

"You were so warm. You felt so safe. I just wanted to feel that for a little while." Gabi lay her head on his chest for a moment remembering that feeling.

"You were so upset. I felt your face above mine, and then you were crying. A tear fell on my face, and I opened my eyes. You were the most beautiful thing I'd ever seen in my life. I reached out for your face, just like the first night you came here and kissed you." Gabi nodded, tears streaming down her cheeks.

"Just like that," she laughed, "minus the dislocation. You held my face so sweetly and kissed me. It was the most amazing kiss in my entire life."

"Me too, baby, me too." Zulu pulled Gabi's face to his own, his lips meeting hers. He kissed her gently, then more forcefully taking her mouth, their tongues in an intimate dance. Gabi leaned up and pulled the sweatshirt and camisole from her body, then shoved Zulu's t-shirt off as well, their bodies now with skin-on-skin contact.

"I need you, Quin," she whispered against his lips. His big hands were splayed across her back, pressing her body into his own, her breasts so beautifully lush and full. One big hand slid down the back of her pajama pants, gripping her ass cheek, kneading it, his long fingers sliding down her crack. Gabi let out a slow moan, and Zulu nearly came in his shorts.

"Get naked, baby," he said into her mouth. She nodded, shoving the waist of her pants down and then wiggling until they were at her ankles. She kicked sideways, sending them across the room, and he laughed. Gabi reached between them and shoved his shorts down, feeling him kick his off as well. Her hand wrapped around his thick cock, and they both moaned together.

Zulu flipped her over once again, pushing one long leg up along the back of the sofa and the other up over his shoulder. He would get seriously deep inside her like this. He smelled her sex and groaned; the tip of his cock smothered in her warmth and wetness.

"Oh, oh God, baby, Quin. I love you so much. I love you, baby," she cried against him.

Yea, he was fucked all kinds of ways to Sunday. He shoved his cock inside her tight hole and waited for her to adjust, but when her rocking hips moved forward faster and faster, he knew his baby needed satisfaction right away.

"Fuuuuckkk, Angel eyes, that is so good, so fucking good, baby," he moaned. She nodded, pulling his head down to her mouth, her tongue gliding along his lips, nibbling on that full lower lip that turned her on big time.

"Quin, Quin, I'm cumming," he nodded, knowing he was right behind her. She arched her back, those perfect snow globes on her chest poking out at him, and he shuddered, his own release spilling inside her. Zulu kissed her sweetly, gently, and then found that she was already moving against his semi-hard cock still inside her.

"Fuck, Angel eyes, you're insatiable," he growled.

"Lucky you," she laughed.

"Fucking right, lucky me, only me."

"Always only you, Quin, always." Gabi flipped him to the floor with a big thud laughing as they hit, then straddling him to ride the next wave of mind-blowing orgasm. When they finally got up to head to the bedroom, they were on orgasm number four, and Gabi still wanted more.

Zulu knew he had more in him, but damn this woman was going to kill him. Maybe he'd talk to Doc about vitamins. But when he looked down to see her lips wrapped around his stiff cock he shook his head. No need for vitamins when you've got this.

CHAPTER THIRTY-THREE

The new Dr. Scott Edwards was a big hit in the emergency room. The nurses thought he was one of the most charming and handsome doctors they'd' seen in a long time, and the other doctors found him intelligent and easy-going. His casual air of confidence and swagger was exactly what they expected from such a skilled surgeon. By the time introductions were done and he'd seen three or four patients, he had phone numbers for every available nurse on the ward.

One nurse especially caught his eyes. Her short brown hair lay in a mass of untamed curls around her face, her lush green eyes filled with passion. She wasn't short, but she wasn't tall either, just average. Her ass was round, leading to full thick thighs, and her tits were nearly his undoing. Even through the scrubs, he could see that her nipples were hard and waiting to be sucked.

As shift ended and he left his coat and stethoscope in his locker, she let a hand glide over his shoulders and smiled.

"Interested in a 'welcome to the city' cocktail," she said, emphasizing the word 'cock.'

"I could be persuaded, Judy," he grinned at the little vixen.

"My place might be closest," she said, smiling at him. He nodded, following her out of the locker room and into the blizzard-like conditions. She wasn't lying that her place was close. Literally within just a few blocks of the hospital.

Scott took the seat offered and watched as she set her things down and excused herself to the back bedroom. A few minutes later, she appeared in nothing but a red lace bra and panty set.

"You weren't really that thirsty, were you?" she smiled.

"Not in the least." He stood and pulled his sweater over his head, then shoved down his pants, his cock bobbing free. Judy shoved him to the sofa, mounting him. "Condom?" he gasped between kisses.

"I'm clean and on the pill. You?" she asked.

"Clean. I always use a condom," he grinned. She nodded, lowering herself on his long thin cock. It wasn't very full, but it was longer than most which made up for the lack of girth. He reached behind her and unhooked the bra, her massive breasts bouncing free, their heavy weight sighing in his hands. He squeezed one roughly, and when she moaned with delight, he squeezed again, biting into the flesh of one.

"Yes, like that, suck my nipples," she demanded. He nodded up at her, taking one big pink nipple in his mouth and sucking hard, biting down with force as she yelped in excitement, all the while seated on his aching cock. He slapped her ass and moved furiously inside her, and she nodded, rocking her body back and forth against him, her huge fleshy breasts slapping him in the chest.

She let out a howl of pleasure as he felt himself release inside her. Before he could even catch his breath, she was on her knees, sucking him off again, getting him hard immediately.

"Greedy, honey?" he laughed.

"You have no idea," she smiled. "I need you to fuck my ass. Can you do that for me?"

"I think I can be persuaded," he grinned. Yea, he could do that for her. The little slut wanted it bad enough he would satisfy her, no problem at all. With his cock now achingly hard between her lips, she knelt in front of him, wiggling her ass toward his cock.

He could only smile as he took a knee behind her, using the juices from her pussy to coat his cock. He slid easily inside her 'not so tight' hole and heard her moan.

"More," she gasped. More? Okay, he thought, more. He slammed into her harder and harder. Reaching under their bodies, he pinched her hard little nub and heard her cry out. His fingers roughly jammed inside her.

"You like that, you little slut?" he asked with a vicious grin.

"Yea, yea, I like that. I'm your slut," she said, breathing heavily, her big tits swinging. Jesus, he got himself a real freak on the first try.

"That's right, my slut," he groaned as he felt his balls tighten and the sweet release inside her ass. She screamed out as her fingers made her cum again. Rolling to her side, she smiled up at him, red marks covering her flesh. She really was delightful, all curves and feminine perfection.

"You're good," she laughed from the floor. He was still kneeling between her legs, his cock already starting to get hard again.

"So are you, my little slut," he grinned. "Suck me. Suck me, and swallow it all."

"Whatever you want," she laughed, "whatever you need, I'm your girl. Afterward, I have some toys in my room. What do you say to a little playtime?"

He grinned down at her as she placed his cock between her lips.

Maybe this new hospital wouldn't be so bad after all. Yea, he could

definitely make this work.

CHAPTER THIRTY-FOUR

For three days, the team was relegated to the property as the blizzard raged outside. Temperatures dipped to sub-zero, and snowdrifts were as high as eight feet in some areas. The trek up their winding road of the mountain was treacherous, and Ghost ordered everyone to stay put until the plows could get through.

Gabi and Zulu took full advantage of the isolation, making their own snowbound honeymoon and unpacking her boxes in their new home together. When the snow finally stopped and the paths and sidewalks were cleared, they were at least able to get to one another on the property. While Zulu and Gunner met at the new gym, Gabi met with Ace on the data he'd been pulling for days.

"I think your instincts were pretty spot on, Angel eyes," said Ace, turning to smile at her. "I did what you asked and started looking at high-profile deaths in the last year and how they might be connected."

"High-profile?" asked Ghost standing in the doorway with Whiskey, Gunner, and Zulu.

"Hey! I thought you guys were going to be down at the gym," she said, smiling at her husband.

"Not much to do in this weather. Now, what do you mean high-profile?" asked Zulu.

"It was something Angel eyes thought about the other night. If all these people were being killed intentionally, who are they, and what is their connection? I started to backtrack to the few we knew about – the three Greeks, the politicians wives, the corporate head – and Angel eyes was spot on. They're all connected," he said, grinning. The four men folded their arms across their chests and stood staring at Ace, waiting for further explanation.

"Oh, ummm," said Gabi, standing up, "so here's what we know. The three Greeks from the same family own Kostas biotech labs. The only surviving family member we can find is the husband; the two politicians wives were the wives of senators on the committee for ethics in medicine, and both served on the FDA's review board; the corporate head who died was head of Libra Pharmaceuticals, a leading manufacturer of vaccines."

"Gabrielle, I appreciate the information, but how the fuck do all these people connect?" asked Ghost.

"I'm getting there," she smiled. "Kostas was working on a biologic that could be used to prevent several strains of deadly viruses, including

Ebola and Marburg, a virus similar to Ebola. In the clinical trials, the biologic worked in the laboratory, but in phase III trials, it was killing patients at an alarming rate, most notably from heart attacks and infections of the lungs. The two senators refused further investigation into the biologic here in the U.S., stating it was too dangerous. Libra, who had agreed to manufacture the vaccine, pulled its licensing agreement, saying the biologic needed more study."

"Okay, so someone killed these people because they were going to manufacture the vaccine?" asked Gunner.

"No. They killed them because they refused to manufacture it and fast-track it to market. We need to find who would benefit most from this and why they would want a biologic that kills instead of prevents the desired disease. It would most likely be someone highly invested in the formulation, maybe a financial backer of the research, or a board member for Libra. The problem is both Libra and Costas are family-owned, privately-held businesses. I, we need to really dig to find the information."

"Holy shit," whispered Zulu. "You're saying that all of these people died because they refused to rush something to market that wasn't ready for mass distribution? Something that would kill everyone it was injected into?"

"That's exactly what I'm saying. And if that's not the case, I think someone wants that biologic for their own uses. We know there were almost a hundred deaths from transplants, and I seriously doubt all were connected to this, but they could have been connected to other things we're unaware of."

"Damn," muttered Ghost. "Why is this shit never easy?"

"I don't know, but I think the quicker we can meet with the senators on the ethics commission, the better. I want to question the senators on what they know, how much information they've been exposed to. I still think it's odd that they suddenly wanted to speak with me, but I'll meet with them. I also think when we show up, you all need to be wearing your kuttes, leather all the way."

"Angel, you know we can't ride our bikes in this weather. As much as we want to, we can't," said Zulu, pulling her in for a hug.

"I know that, but if you guys show up with me dressed like bikers, not ex-Special Forces, whoever we're meeting with will think you're just a bunch of motorheads or gang members. They won't know what I know about all of you," she smiled.

"And what is it you know about us, Angel eyes?" asked Ace with small grin.

"That you're all highly intelligent, well-educated, critical thinking, badass men. I'd trust you anywhere with me, but they don't know that. All they will know is I sought refuge with the club, and I'm trying to find out where all these bodies were going."

Whiskey grinned at her and turned to the other men in the room. "Dr. Angel eyes thinks we're smart. Thank you, Angel."

"You're welcome," she laughed. "But it's the truth. I'm going to guess that you guys are underestimated all the time, which may very well play in your favor. I would think it does anyway."

"It does indeed," smiled Ghost.

"Okay, so we think all of this is tying back to this one thing being approved and used as a vaccine, is that right?" asked Gunner.

"Yes." They looked at her as if asking for more information or clarity, and she stood. "Listen, a vaccine brought to market can generate billions of dollars in revenue for a company. If I own stock or have partial ownership, the possibilities are endless. Someone could simply be trying to get this to market, only to sell it to another pharmaceutical company."

"Alright, so basically, you want to see what these two senators know, and we just play your muscle, is that right?" asked Gunner.

"For now," she smiled, "yes. I'm going to do some more digging here. I just have a feeling we're missing something, something really important. I need to ask all the right questions to see what they really know about this. I promise I won't do anything stupid, but I have to figure out if these two people know anything at all. I-I have some questions, some tactics that might come out of left field, but I'm asking that you all trust me on this."

"I don't know either of them," said Zulu, "you, Ghost? Whiskey?" Both men shook their heads. Gunner shrugged, not saying anything. "We'll trust you, Gabi, but if you put yourself or any of us in danger, we step in." She nodded, smiling at the group.

"Alright, Angel eyes," said Zulu. "We play your muscle, and you play the brain, easy."

"Also," said Ace, "two more things before you guys leave. ERG Industries is just a shell corporation. There is nothing on them, absolutely nothing, and believe me, I searched. Their address is somewhere in Idaho, and when I google it, it's just an empty warehouse. There are no cars parked outside it, nothing. Only a sign with ERG painted on it."

"The funeral home didn't admit to anything at first, but a few hours later called me back to say that one of their drivers admitted to taking cash from a man to pick up bodies from the morgue and cremate them. The driver was fired, but he didn't have a name, only a description which matches what you gave us for the guy who beat you."

"Okay," she said, letting out a breath, "unanswered questions, got it."

CHAPTER THIRTY-FIVE

Old Ebbitt Grille is a staple in downtown D.C. Politicians rubbed elbows with diplomats; the rich and famous ate side-by-side with the average Joe; the food was superb; the drinks were inventive, and the location was prime real estate. The atmosphere was old-world charm and elegance meets a neighborhood pub. Gabi knew that the dress code quite possibly could be an issue for the guys all dressed in their leather, but she was willing to take a gamble and push the limits.

The streets were surprisingly clear of snow and ice, although in fairness, the D.C. area didn't get as much as their little mountain community. Traffic was light overall, but still more than any of them were used to. As they passed the Lincoln Memorial, Gabi bent her head slightly to look out the window as Zulu and Gunner grinned at her childlike expression.

"Have you never been, Angel eyes?" asked Zulu.

"No. I've never seen any of the monuments. Every time I was in the city, it was to work or attend a conference or school. There just never seemed to be enough time to see the things I wanted to see. I lived in Baltimore as a kid, a train ride away, yet every time there was a school trip here, my parents made excuses for me not to come, worried that I would get separated from the group or lost."

"I promise we'll make time, baby," said Zulu, kissing her temple. "When all this is over, we'll come in and spend a few days visiting all the sites." She smiled, nodding like a little kid, and he could only chuckle at her enthusiasm.

"Okay, Angel eyes," said Whiskey, pulling up to the valet. The young man stood at the door, and he gave him a look that clearly communicated he wanted him to back the hell up. "Our contact is already inside with the two senators. Remember, we don't leave your side. If you get up to take a piss, one of the boys will follow. We let you take the lead on this."

"Understood," she said solemnly. Whiskey opened the door to the SUV and handed the keys to the valet who eyed the big man up and down, his thick beard and long hair along with all the leather a contrast to the usual patrons. The twins entered the restaurant first, followed by Gabi, Zulu, Whiskey, and Gunner. The hostess looked up with an open mouth and then back down quickly, nervously glancing over her shoulder for the manager.

"We have a reservation," said Gabi. "We're meeting Senators Kantek and Jette."

"Ummm, yes, I see that here. We just usually have a dress code," she said quietly as if the guys didn't know exactly what she was saying.

"Well, since you're slow, and it's the lunch crowd, and the senators are waiting, I would think you could make an exception this time," said Gabi.

"Right, follow me," said the hostess with a haughty air. She led them to the back of the restaurant to one of the private rooms, which only made Gabi glare at the girl even more. If they were in a private room, what in the hell did it matter how they were dressed.

"Dr. London?" asked a tall, middle-aged man in a suit with an outstretched hand. She didn't bother to correct him, only nodding.

"Yes, that's me."

"I'm Senator Andrew Jette, and this is my colleague." He didn't get to utter another syllable.

"Senator Gail Kantek. And who is your entourage? I believe our meeting was with you and only you," she asked, looking each of the men up and down. Another man stood and shook hands with Whiskey.

"As I told you, Senator, Dr. London was attacked, and these men belong to a motorcycle club that's helping to protect her." The woman gave a loud 'hurumph' and took her seat, followed by Gabi and then the men.

"Agent Mathers tells us that you've uncovered some disturbing trends around all these deaths with the transplants," said Senator Jette.

"Yes, sir," she said calmly. "I guess let me start at the beginning." Gabi told the story of discovering the bodies and then her beating, finding her way to the motorcycle club, randomly, of course. She didn't tell them of her relationship with Zulu or her knowledge of the links with the deaths, and as she'd directed, none of the guys said a word.

Senator Kantek glared in her direction, making Gabi squirm a bit at first. She actually wanted the senator to underestimate her, to believe that she could bully her; it was all part of her plan. Yet, there was something about her stare that made her very uncomfortable.

"Dr. London do you have any experience at all in organ transplant?" asked Kantek in a condescending tone.

"No, ma'am, I do not. But I am an emergency room surgeon specializing in trauma. I recognize when a body has been harvested, and more than that, I recognize that some of these individuals were not ideal candidates."

"Just how would you know that, Dr. London?" she poked. Gabi could feel Zulu stiffen next to her. It was barely perceptible, but she felt it, and so did the other men.

"These bodies were victims, ma'am. They were not in ideal health, but they definitely should have survived an organ donation. In fact, in the case of the bodies in Sacramento, it appears their bodies were dumped before their death. According to two surviving family members, their loved one was promised cash for their organs and then were left for dead." The woman leaned back in her chair, just staring at Gabi. She felt those eyes seep into her soul and knew that they were not kind eyes. She also knew that she wouldn't back down from this woman. She couldn't, knowing what she discovered earlier in the day.

"Dr. London?" Jette was finally taking his turn to speak. "Agent Mathers said that you believed a Dr. Gary Scott was responsible for the organ harvesting, is that right?"

"Dr. Scott and another man I didn't know attacked me. He is the only individual with that kind of access at the hospital, and he got very angry with me when he found me looking at the records in the morgue. Unfortunately, when I went back to locate the records again, they were wiped from the system."

"So, you have no evidence?" asked Kantek with an evil grin. "You want us to launch some sort of full-scale investigation based on your hunch that a respectable surgeon is harvesting organ. Do I have that right?"

Gabi stared directly into the woman's face, not saying a word. She let her eyes make the woman uncomfortable, her glare unable to look away from Gabi.

"No, Senator, I don't expect you to take my word for it. I expect you to call South Atlanta General and find out that he left without notice. Dr. Gary Scott is in the wind. Technically, he doesn't even exist. He uses different identities, different credentials for every hospital. Now, I'm not in the FBI like Agent Mathers. I have no policing skills. Hell, I barely know how to type my notes into the hospital computers, but I know enough that someone would have to have serious skills to get that kind of identification quickly with all the necessary documentation and paperwork."

Senator Kantek squirmed slightly in her seat, crossing one leg over the other, casually turning her spoon over several times.

"My question is, who would have that kind of power, Senator? Hmmm? Who would be able to make that kind of paperwork appear out of thin air, get a doctor assigned to a hospital so quickly, no questions asked? Who would have that sort of unquestionable power? Perhaps someone with ties to the medical and pharmaceutical community. Maybe a group like ERG, Emergency Response Group, claiming they specialize in emergency transplants. Of course, no one can find that they've ever aided in that kind of operation, but what do I know? Then again, would that make sense to you, Agent Mathers?"

Gabi continued to stare directly at Senator Kantek, the woman's face so red she thought she might have a stroke. Jette continued to watch the interaction but said nothing, only looking from one face to the other, but it was the men behind her who let a slow lazy grin appear on their sweet lips, and they all looked down at Angel eyes. Gotcha.

"I assure you I have no idea who would be able to provide that kind of documentation, Dr. London. And I have no clue who this ERG is. It seems a rather elaborate scheme only to obtain organs that were unusable," she casually waved a hand in the air, and Gabi smiled at her once more.

"I didn't say they were unusable, Senator." Gabi's face was without expression, her tone calm and controlled.

"Y-you said they were homeless, drug addicts. That would imply their organs cannot be used," she said with a huff.

"No. I didn't say that at all. I said they weren't ideal candidates. Where on earth would you get the idea they were drug users? Homeless? Interesting," said Gabi. The woman stood, shoving her chair backwards.

"We're not done, Senator. Sit." Gabi's voice was commanding, and even Gunner had to admit his dick jumped a bit at her forceful tone.

"How dare you speak to me in that tone!" she huffed. "I'm a respected doctor in my field as well, young lady, specializing in internal medicine; I'm a senior senator for the United States of America! I am on three very important committees, including medical ethics, Dr. London. Something you should remember!"

"Are you threatening me, Senator Kantek?" smiled Gabi. "No, don't answer that. My record is impeccable. I have nothing to worry about. You're right. You are a senior senator for the good old U.S. of A.

However, Kantek isn't your real name, is it? In fact, it's your third husband's name. Your maiden name is Kostas. Your family owns Kostas Biomedical, don't they?"

"Wh-what, how did you know that?" she murmured, slumping in her chair.

"I'm good at my work, Senator. A doctor needs to have friends in all the right places, good investigative skills to get to the real problem. Your great-grandparents were Angela and Dmitri Kostas, both highly respected, brilliant biochemists. They started Kostas more than fifty years ago with your father. Your brother inherited the company after your father's tragic death in a boating accident. An accident that was never investigated."

"H-how…" Gabi held up a hand to stop her.

"Your brother is, forgive me, was married to Elena Mantzania. She, unfortunately, had a genetic kidney disease, which she passed on to her two daughters. How am I doing so far, Senator?" She waited, but the woman said nothing. "Never mind, that was rhetorical. Your sister-in-law and two nieces all needed kidney transplants. You needed the biologic to pass all trials. I mean, as someone who owns forty-nine percent of the company, you would be an extremely wealthy woman. Of course, your brother has ethics and morals. He refused, didn't he? You, of course, decided that you would promise him something he didn't think was possible – life for his family."

Kantek looked at the faces of the angry men seated around the table. Their eyes boring holes into her from across the room. Jette moved his seat away from her, his face repulsed by the words coming from Gabi.

"You promised your own sister-in-law, your own nieces' life. Of course, with them dead, you would have the majority of the company. It seems your brother gifted his wife five percent of the company on their marriage. Unheard of, really, but that meant that with her dead and the nieces dead, you controlled the majority. That five percent would go to the board, leaving your brother with only forty-six percent. You would hold all power."

"This is absurd! You have no clue what you're talking about! I'm leaving," she said, standing from the chair.

"Not yet," said Mathers, shoving her back into the seat. "I think I'd like to hear the end of this story." Gabi smiled at the man and nodded.

"So, your brother acquiesced. Gave you what you wanted, but then the problem was Libra. I mean, damn, you needed more family members sitting on important boards. Then a gift landed in your lap. The CEO of Libra needed a liver transplant. You promised him life for a majority share and final say in the distribution rights for new vaccines. Quite a feat actually, but then again, family-owned businesses have more freedom for these things."

"You're despicable," said Jette, staring at the woman.

"The thing I can't quite figure out yet," said Gabi calmly, picking an imaginary piece of lint from her jeans, "is why this elaborate scheme. Why not just poison them or put a bullet in their heads?"

Kantek sat across from the cocky doctor, staring her down. How? How had she discovered everything they so carefully planned out? Did that idiot surgeon spill the beans?

"You think you're so smart. You think you have all the answers. You don't. You and your freakish eyes and hair. That's right, I knew about your features from Gary or whatever he's going by now. He owed me money, lots of it, so he was easy pickings. As you well know, doctor, organ harvesting is big business, and it was my perfect little side business until this vaccine was approved. When my idiot brother pulled it, I knew I had to do something. There it was, staring me in the face. My business was already good. I was just going to make it better."

"You killed your nieces, little girls with their entire lives ahead of them. Your own sister-in-law, thereby destroying your brother. You took the life of a man who had a wife, children, and grandchildren at home, and so many more. Your greed is despicable! You claim to honor the ethics and morality of medicine. You're nothing but a backstreet butcher. You're no better than some quack performing abortions on innocent little girls with rusty instruments. I don't know what the penalty is for your crimes, but I hope they give you the maximum possible sentence."

"You won't stop it," she said with a snide grin. "You might take me down, but there will be a hundred more in my place. It's no different than the drug trade or weapons or human trafficking. There will always be someone else to take my place at the table."

"That may be, *Gail,* because I damned sure won't call you senator, but you will be in a jail cell eating pudding and boxed mashed potatoes made by an angry woman named Madge, whose own husband died from a transplant. And she will know what you did."

The horror on Kantek's face said it all. She hadn't thought past her greed, past her own need for money and fame. Her own arrogance made her believe she would never be caught.

Mathers stood and handcuffed her, reading her rights, and then led her away from the table.

"I'm not sure how you knew all of that," said Senator Jette, "but we could sure use someone like you on our team." Gabi laughed, holding up both hands in surrender.

"Oh no, not me. I'm a surgeon. More importantly, I'm a wife and hope to start a family of my own one day soon. I do not need to be a politician as well. However, I will help you with this case if you need assistance going through the data." He smiled at the young woman and nodded, shaking her hand.

"I may take you up on that, Dr. London," he said, grinning.

"It's Dr. Slater," she smiled. He only nodded, leaving them all in the private dining room. Gabi turned to see five very serious faces staring her down. Three had their arms crossed over their chests, and two had their hands planted at their hips.

"What?"

CHAPTER THIRTY-SIX

"So, you're telling me that you knew all this information this morning and decided to not say anything to any of us?" asked Ghost on the other end of the call.

"Well, yes and no," she grinned.

"Which is it, Angel eyes, yes or no?" asked Zulu.

"I knew most of it. Honestly, I wasn't sure how I was going to confront her with it. I knew that her family, owned Kostas, and I thought maybe she was a victim in all this. I looked up both of the senators last night. Jette was so squeaky clean I almost thought he would be the dirty one. Turns out he's as squeaky as he looks. She was harder."

"How so?" asked Gunner.

"It was like a lot of stops and starts in her history. I would find her education information, and then it would go blank for five years. Then it was a marriage and her husband's death. Then another marriage, he was a senator, and she took over his seat when he died. Then another marriage. It was just so much and so odd that no one thought to look into her further.

"I watched this speech she gave at her alma mater, and it was so cold, so distant. I just knew she was hiding something. I didn't know until I sat in front of her what I was going to say. When she buried herself by saying the victims were addicts and homeless, I knew I had her."

"You sure you're not a fed?" asked Whiskey.

"Pretty sure," she said, laughing. "What do we do about Gary or whoever he is?"

"We've got that," said Mathers, stepping back into the room. "I've sent the black widow with a couple of my colleagues to FBI headquarters. We'll interrogate her once again, but I heard enough to put her under, and with your testimony and the evidence, she'll get life for sure. I sent a team to pick up the doctor and his muscle. They should be back at HQ by the time I get there."

"Is it over for her?" asked Zulu.

"I wish I could say yes, brother, but I would say keep her close and locked down until we're sure we have everyone. We'll need to get the brother back here from Greece, get someone connected with Libra to give any testimony they can. I know the two senators who lost their wives will be seeing this to the end as well."

"It's all so sad," said Gabi. "I mean, all for money. Money that she possessed anyway. How much did she think she needed?"

"No telling," said Mathers. "I've seen a lot of fucked up shit in my job, so unfortunately, nothing surprises me anymore. I'll let you folks go. I'll come up your way if I need anything." Zulu nodded, shaking the man's hand as they left the restaurant.

"What do you say we stop and say hello to Lincoln?" said Gunner, smiling.

"Really?!" Gabi jumped with excitement. "Thank you!" Whiskey drove the SUV around the mall until he found a parking spot. Stepping from the vehicle, the group worked their way toward the long pool, first stopping at the WWII memorial, then the Vietnam Memorial, then the Korean War memorial. At each one, she sensed their somber, respectful tone.

Gunner spotted several older veterans standing near the Vietnam memorial wall and walked up, striking up a conversation. It was as if he recognized their bearing. Both were marines, and he immediately started chatting with them, waving the rest of the group over. Thirty minutes later, they shook hands, saluted the wall, and parted ways.

"That was so kind of all of you to speak to those men," said Gabi.

"It wasn't kindness, Angel eyes, it was respect; it was decency; it was just the right fucking thing to do," said Zulu. She only nodded as they took the steps one at a time toward the massive seated figure of Abraham Lincoln. Gabi stopped and read the words.

Four score and seven years ago our fathers brought forth on this continent, a new nation, conceived in Liberty, and dedicated to the proposition that all men are created equal.

Now we are engaged in a great civil war, testing whether that nation, or any nation so conceived and so dedicated, can long endure. We are met on a great battle-field of that war. We have come to dedicate a portion of that field, as a final resting place for those who here gave their lives that that nation might live. It is altogether fitting and proper that we should do this.

But, in a larger sense, we cannot dedicate -- we cannot consecrate -- we cannot hallow -- this ground. The brave men, living and dead, who struggled here, have consecrated it, far above our poor power to add or detract. The world will little note, nor long remember what we say here, but it can never forget what they did here. It is for us the living, rather, to be dedicated here to the unfinished work which they who fought here have thus far so nobly advanced. It is rather for us to be here dedicated to the great task remaining before us -- that from these honored dead we take increased devotion to that cause for which they gave the last full measure of devotion -- that we here highly resolve that these dead shall not have died in vain -- that this nation, under God, shall have a new birth of freedom -- and that government of the people, by the people, for the people, shall not perish from the earth.

Abraham Lincoln
November 19, 1863

"That these dead shall not have died in vain…" whispered Gabi. "I hope that's true for the people I found as well." The men nodded in her direction, taking their time walking back to the car. By the time they pulled into the compound, it was nearly ten o'clock. As they said their goodbyes, Ace poked his head out of his office space.

"Well?" he asked. Gabi looked at him and nodded, a small triumphant grin on her face.

"Guilty."

CHAPTER THIRTY-SEVEN

Three days later, Mathers showed up at Club Steel, asking to meet with the team who had been present in D.C. Seated at one of the dining tables, he finally spoke.

"Kantek killed herself in her cell yesterday. The only thing she did right was left a note explaining why she did it. She definitely wanted money and control of Kostas Biomedical, but she also said she wanted mankind to suffer. Not sure why. She could have just been a stone-cold bitch."

"I wish I could say I was relieved, but I'm not," said Gabi. "I wanted that woman to face a trial and public ridicule. Is that wrong of me?"

"Not wrong, Angel eyes," said Zulu, kissing his wife.

"Fishbein and his muscle were both caught last night. Karl was counting his cash on the bed in his hotel room. Idiot had more than three million in cash in a bag locked in his hotel safe. Fishbein wasn't much better. Caught him with a nurse in the supply closet at the hospital. Let's just say I saw more of that man than I wanted to. He'll be tried for negligence, murder, attempted murder, yada, yada, yada."

"Yada?" scowled Gunner.

"Yea, too many things to list out, brother. We're not sure how the other deaths were connected to the biologic or if they even were. Kantek was a vicious woman with a lot of enemies. My guess is she figured out how to hurt people in the worst way. Coroner exhumed two of the bodies and found out that they were former rivals of hers from college. Doubt they had anything to do with this. She just was getting revenge."

"God, that's awful," said Gabi, gripping her stomach as it pitched forward. "I think I need a ginger ale or something."

"I'll get it, Angel eyes," said Hawk.

"What do you need from me?" she asked Mathers.

"Nothing right now. We may need you to give a deposition, possibly testify against Fishbein and Karl, but we won't know for a while. Wheels of justice move slowly, no shit about that." She nodded as Hawk placed the drink in front of her.

"Well, we were glad to help with this," said Ghost. "If you need anything else from us, let us know."

"Yea, just a question. How did you guys find all that information? I mean, even my team didn't find that shit." Gabi looked up, and stone-faced replied.

"I'm just really good with research." She saw Ace out of the corner of her eye, standing off to the side, but never once looked directly at him. Mathers nodded, grinning, and waved as he left. Ace walked slowly, finally standing in front of Gabi and grinned.

"I think I might like another hug, Angel eyes," he said, holding out his arms. She stood slowly and wrapped her arms around him, smelling the mushroom burger he'd had at lunch. She felt it coming.

"Oh God!" She held a hand over her mouth and ran, disappearing to the back.

CHAPTER THIRTY-EIGHT

"Gabi! Gabi, are you okay?" asked Zulu pounding on the ladies' room door. "Gabi, I'm coming in."

"I'm okay," she said, leaning over the toilet. "I'm okay."

"Honey, you don't look okay. You're paler than usual, and I heard you puking. Are you sick? Do we need to get Doc to take a look?"

"No. I think I know what's wrong," she said, smiling. He gave her a blank stare, shaking his head. "Quin, we've been fucking like rabbits for more than a month without protection. What do you think is wrong?"

"You-you're pregnant?" he murmured. "You-you're gonna have my baby. My baby..."

"That's right, big guy," she said, rinsing her mouth in the sink. "I'm having your baby."

"Fuck yea!" he screamed. The laughter of his brothers outside the bathroom could be heard with Gunner proudly saying.

"Everyone owes me twenty. Angel eyes was pregnant within six weeks."

It didn't take long to confirm that she was indeed pregnant. Three pregnancy tests later and a visit to an obstetrician confirmed it all. Zulu was immediately in hyper-protective mode with her. Barring her from climbing, walking fast, dancing, or doing anything other than sitting.

She put a stop to that quickly. As morning sickness took over her body, Grace swelled with her pregnancy, and they commiserated on their bloated bodies.

By April, Gabi's morning sickness was gone, but she was huge already and knew she shouldn't be that big. On the way to the doctor, Grace tagging along, they quickly diverted to the hospital when Grace's water broke. Gabi made the calls to Ghost and Zulu, who immediately gathered everyone to head to the hospital.

Five hours later, Jack Tyran was born. Eight pounds and four ounces of precious boy. Eagle cried, holding his godson, and Doc argued that he would be the favored godfather. As the doctor confirmed all was good with Grace, she encouraged Gabi to follow her to another room for her scheduled sonogram.

More than thirty minutes later, Zulu was starting to panic when Gabi walked in the room with red-rimmed eyes and a ghostly-white face.

"Baby? Angel eyes, what's wrong? Is everything okay?" he asked, pulling her next to him on the sofa in Grace's room. She nodded, crying once more.

"We-we're having twins," she said quietly. She looked up at Grace, sadness filling her face.

"Oh, honey," said Grace. "Come here, Gabi. Come over here." Gabi sat on the edge of the bed, and Grace pulled her into a big hug, letting her cry it out against her chest.

"Listen to me, Gabi, I'm so happy for you. So very, very happy that I get to share in the joy you'll have with your twins. I am so blessed with this little boy. I promise you. Your joy does not intensify my sadness at having lost my daughters. They're watching over us, all of us. You are going to be an amazing mom, and we'll do this together." She kissed Gabi on the forehead and hugged her once again.

"We're having twins," whispered Zulu again.

"Yes, big, huge, twins," she grimaced. "The doctor... the doctor said they might get as big as seven pounds each! I'm going to hate you, Quin, seriously hate you!" The entire room erupted in laughter, and Eagle continued to rock his godson, and Whiskey watched his friend drown in happiness. Kat leaned toward him and whispered.

"What do you say you and I try for one of those?" she said. He looked down at her with a sharp twist of his head and grinned.

"Hell to the fucking yea, baby. Hell yea!"

CHAPTER THIRTY-NINE

By summer, JT, as Jack Tyran had become known, was a healthy bouncing baby boy keeping his parents on their toes. Grace, the far more experienced parent, took everything in stride, relishing in this gift of being a parent again.

Gabi was huge, literally looking like she could give birth at any moment. She was only at thirty-two weeks but was already on bed rest with Zulu waiting on her hand and foot. Because he had to be at the gym, he installed cameras so he could watch her all day, calling her to fuss if she got out of bed.

Kat and Whiskey were trying for their offspring, maybe a little too much, but enjoying the process, nevertheless.

Gunner tried to limit his exposure to the eternal marital bliss cloud that hung over the club. He had a full slate of clients at the gym and no time for all the couples bullshit being thrust in his direction.

Many of his clients were women who wanted a chance to flaunt their bodies in front of the single muscle-bound marine. He never mixed business and pleasure, always politely turning them down. Most were married, which made him feel sorry for their husbands. Some were just lonely widows or divorcees. His favorites were two seventy-year-old sisters who made him laugh and brought him cookies.

This morning he was interviewing a new client who wanted to not only be in better shape but also wanted to learn to fight. He would handle the physical fitness and let Zulu train her for the fighting, although he was capable of doing it all.

It was a strange call when she contacted him yesterday. She seemed nervous and unsure of what she even wanted, sounding seriously distracted. It took every ounce of patience he had to get her to answer his questions and finally tell him that she simply wanted to become more physically fit and learn to fight.

He suspected those weren't her only reasons, but he would give that to her for now. He looked at the clock and noted that she was already a few minutes late, not something he tolerated. Walking back toward his office, he checked his phone to be sure she hadn't called and cancelled.

As he walked back to the front desk, his heart stopped in his chest. Nothing, nothing could prepare him for the woman standing in front of him. Wearing a body-hugging floral summer dress and strappy high-heeled sandals, she had short black hair cut in a severe bob, falling to the tops of her shoulders. Her eyes were an exotic almond shape, the rich brown framed by thick, full black lashes. Her mouth was full and pouty, the red lips so luscious he shifted to move his hardening dick to the side.

Her skin was the color of honey like liquid gold. Judging by his six-foot-two, she was probably five-feet-five, but she was all lush fucking curves, from her full breasts to her tapered waist down to the scrumptious hips and thick thighs. Holy fucking hell, he'd just sighted a goddess.

"Hello?" she said, waving a hand in front of his face. "Did you get yourself a good look? It's not polite to stare, you know."

"Sorry, beautiful, but we don't get a lot of gorgeous women in here," he said, giving her his best sexy smile. She looked around the room and gave him a perturbed look, waving her arm in a big circle.

"You have an entire gym full of beautiful women, all staring at you, slick," she said sarcastically. "I'm here to meet with Gunner Michaels. Can you let him know that Darby Greer is here?"

Lucky fucking stars are in my sky. Son-of-a-bitch, this is my new client? I need to keep my dick in my pants long enough to get to know this woman.

"You're in luck. I'm Gunner Michaels," he said, smiling down at her, his big arms flexing as he reached out his hand to shake hers. She looked at him, her gaze perusing up and down his deliciously muscular body, her mouth opening and closing.

"Nope, no, thank you," she said, turning and walking out the door.

"What the hell was that?"

OTHER BOOKS BY MARY KENNEDY YOU

MIGHT ENJOY!

REAPER Security Series
Erin's' Hero
Lauren's Warrior
Lena's' Mountain
Sara's' Chance
Mary's Angel
Kari's Gargoyle
Rachelle's Savior
Adele's Heart
Tori's' Secret
Finding Lily
Montana Rules
Savannah Rain
Gray Skies
My First Choice
Three Wishes
Second Chances
One Day at a Time
When You Least Expect It
Missing Hearts
Trail of Love

My SEAL Boys (connections to the REAPER Series)
Ian
Noa
Carter
Lars
Trevor
Fitz
Chris
O'Hara

Strange Gifts Series
Dark Visions
Dark Medicine
Dark Flame

Steel Patriots MC Series
Ghost – Book One
Doc – Book Two
Whiskey – Book Three

ABOUT THE AUTHOR

Mary Kennedy is the mother of two adult children, has an amazing son-in-law, and is grandmother to two beautiful grandsons. She works full-time at a job she loves, and writing is her creative outlet. She lives in Texas and enjoys traveling, reading, and cooking. Her passion for assisting veterans and veteran causes comes from a strong military family background. Mary loves to hear from her readers and encourages them to join her mailing list, as she'll keep you up-to-date on new releases at https://insatiableink.squarespace.com. You can also join her Facebook page at Insatiable Ink.

Dear Readers,

I love hearing from you and encourage you to visit my website Insatiable Ink. Leave me know your thoughts and ideas on new books or expanding on characters. It's also a safe space to give your own feelings, like those of the characters. I love reading about how you relate to the stories because as we all know, there's a little of each of them within us.

I look forward to hearing from you and hope you enjoy other books in my collections.

Explore… and enjoy!